PROMISED LAND

By Simeon G. Silverio, Jr.

Published by the:
Asian Journal San Diego
*The original and first
Asian Journal in America*
E-Mail: asianjournal@aol.com

Published by the:
Asian Journal San Diego
The original and first Asian Journal in America
Simeon G. Silverio, Jr.*, Editor & Publisher*
E-Mail: sandiegoasianjournal@yahoo.com

1st Printing, 2011

The stories in this book were originally published in
The Asian Journal San Diego in 2010

Cover Photo: Sunrise in San Felipe, Baja California, Mexico

*Lovingly dedicated to
my beloved parents and family*

Table of Contents

1

Her U.S. Navy Dreamboat

"*Eto na ang tubig mo*, Miss Beautiful (Here's your water)," Lando told his girlfriend Isabel as he brought a huge container of water into the *batalan* (an open air washroom made of bamboo) of her house in Gagalangin, Tondo, Manila. He poured the water into a huge clay pot, a "tapayan".

"Thanks," she said with a sweet smile.

It was a hot Monday morning. Isabel needed to take a bath before going to school. Her family's house had no bathroom; instead, they bathed in the *batalan* at the back. The floor of the *batalan* was made of bamboo cut in half and laid side by side. To take a bath, one scooped up water from the *tapayan* with a *tabo*, a half-gallon metal container made from a can of coffee. Hot water was a luxury, if not a fantasy. One must heat water on the stove and mix it with the cold liquid in a container for a hot bath.

The water flowed down the head or body and dripped through the openings of the bamboo floor down to the ground. Isabel's house, however, did not sit on a ground but instead on a body of water. A wooden pedestrian bridge connected it to the shore. It was one of the houses built in that part of Tondo in the 1950s by people who did not own any land. They were the original squatters before squatting became fashionable in the city.

The pedestrian bridge had been a problem before. The family's first child, while a toddler, was able to get out of the house, walked on the bridge, and fell in the water below, drowning tragically. Anybody who had experienced such a tragedy would move out of the house as it would remind them of the death of the child. However, the family was too poor to do so. Everyday they walked on the bridge and their hearts would grieve, but they could not do anything but endure their suffering until time erased the bitter memory in their mind, healing the wound.

A five-foot high wall made of bamboo surrounded the roofless *batalan*. A wooden ladder was placed on an open doorway and attached to a wooden walkway on the side of the house. Since it was an open-air setting, people bathed with their clothes still on. The girls scrubbed their bodies with soap by inserting their hands through their necklines and sleeves. To rinse their bodies, they poured water through their necklines. The men and boys simply wore shorts. Isabel had never experienced taking a shower in her entire life and had never before bathed in the nude. They changed clothes inside the only room of the house, the "silid." It was not very private; for example, the doorway had only a curtain instead of doors to block the view from the outside. The family members slept alongside each other in the living room on a huge mat and under a mosquito net. The still water around them was a breeding ground for mosquitoes, which buzzed around and bit their skin if they slept outside the net.

Their toilet was an outhouse about 100 feet away from the main house. It was made of bamboo just like the *batalan*, with openings on the floor through which stools and urine fell into the water below. This was somewhat

8

convenient as they never had any drainage problems. It was connected from the *batalan* by a bamboo walkway with a guide post on the side. In the evening, when it was dark and no one could see them, they simply urinated through the *batalan*'s bamboo floor.

Isabel's family was not the poorest of the poor, but they were poor alright. Her father worked as a clerk in the City Hall while her mother stayed home. Isabel had a younger brother and a sister. As homeowners, they were able to save on rent. Isabel's maternal great grandparents had built the home years ago, and it had since been passed on from generation to generation. They were in no danger of being evicted because the city's elected officials turned a blind eye on their violations because they needed the votes of those like them. Since she became aware of their situation in life, Isabel had long dreamed of living in a decent apartment one day, just like some of her classmates.

"O, alis ka na at maliligo na ako (You can go now and I will take a bath)", Isabel told Lando who was mischievously smiling at her.

"Puwede bang makapanood muna ng 'wet look' (Can I watch a wet look)?" he asked.

The phrase was popular from a movie featuring sexy Filipina movie stars coming out from the sea, their naked bodies almost visible through their wet attire.

She scooped water from the *tapayan* and threw it at Lando .

"O, panoorin mo ang 'wet look' mo (Here, watch your own wet look)," she told her boyfriend who was laughing as he scampered away.

THEIR HOUSE HAD NO RUNNING WATER INSIDE. Ever since Lando became her boyfriend, she never had to fetch water from the public faucet on the side of the street before taking a bath; rather, he did it for her. In return, they would occasionally make out in public parks and, if they could afford it, on the rear seats of the dark part of a movie theater's balcony.

Lando was her classmate from elementary to high school. When they were in third year of high school, he began courting her as they walked home from school. He was attractive and funny, and it was just a matter of time before she returned his affections.

However, she was using her heart instead of her head, at least according to her friend Wilma.

"Ano ang mapapala mo diyan? Wala kang kinabukasan diyan (What will you get from him? You have no future with him!)," she often told Isabel. *"Mahirap ka na nga, kukuha ka pa ng mas mahirap sa daga* (You are already poor and still you will get somebody poorer than a rat)!"

Wilma was right, but Isabel was not yet thinking of settling down. She dreamed of one day earning her college degree, finding a good job, or even going abroad just like her cousin Ditas. Ditas, the daughter of her mom's sister, *Tiya* (Auntie) Lucing, grew up in abject poverty in the province. Her father passed away when she was ten. *Tiya* Lucing used to go to Manila to borrow money from her sister just to tide them over. Having married a neighbor who had joined the United States Navy, Ditas moved to San Diego, California while her mother and siblings stayed in the province. Now it was Lucing who occasionally sent money to Isabel's mother.

One time, Isabel's mother got mad at her sister for not sending the needed funds.

"Butas butas na ang bubong namin, tumutulo na pag umuulan. Hindi man lamang ako pinahiram (Our roof is already full of holes. It is leaking whenever it rains. She didn't even lend me money)," Isabel's mother complained.

"Baka naman kinakapos din. Alam mo naman sa Amerika, hirap din si Ditas at marami silang gastos (She may be short of money. You know in America, people are also having a hard time, and they have many expenses)," Isabel's father comforted his wife.

"Hu, ang kapatid kong iyan, mula nang makapag-asawa ng U.S. Navy ang anak, naging matayog na (That sister of mine. Ever since her daughter married a U.S. Navy personnel, she has become aloof)."

"Ikaw kasi, eh (It's because of you)," Isabel's father reminded his wife. *"Naging matapobre ka sa kanila* (You have been snobbish)."

"Kailan ako naging matapobre (When have I been snobbish)?"

"Remember the time when you caught Lucing's children eating star apples during your visit there?"

Lucing and her sister inherited the yard in the province wherein Lucing's house sat from their parents. Its produce, the coconuts, the santols, the macopas and the star apples were equally divided between them. During one of her visits, however, Isabel's mom berated her nephews and niece for eating star apples.

"Pasensiya ka na ate, nagugutom ang mga bata (Forgive them sister, the children are hungry)."

"*Hu, mga patay gutom ang mga anak mo* (Your children are hungry as dogs)." This was a mean thing to say, so mean it created a wide rift between the sisters.

But now the tables would be turned as Lucing's family was presently providing help to her sister. Isabel's mom always thought her younger sister was getting even at her whenever she could not provide help.

"YOU MUST JOIN THE U.S. NAVY so we can live abroad," Isabel often told her boyfriend Lando as they walked in the park, weaving dreams for their future together. He would just shrug his shoulders in response.

"*Mahirap doon, maglalampaso ako ng paluhod sa sahig ng barko. Magtatanggal ako ng kalawang sa gilid, baka mahulog pa ako. Hindi ako marunong lumangoy* (It is hard there. I will have to scrub the deck of the ship on my knees. I will have to remove rusts from the sides of the ships. I might fall. I don't even know how to swim)."

But Isabel was persistent. She knew his joining the Navy was her only way out of poverty. And if Lando would not follow her wish, then she was ready to replace him with somebody who would.

In the meantime, they were still young, and he had plenty of time to mature and realize the logic of her plan.

2

Colorful Jeepneys and God's Blessings

After bathing and dressing, Isabel walked out of the house along the wooden pathway that led into an alley way and a street. Near the corner, she saw her boyfriend Lando naked from the waist up. He was filling up containers of water in a public faucet with his friends.

"Hello Miss Beautiful," his friends teased her.

"*Ang suwerte mo* (You are lucky)," one of them told the smiling Lando.

Isabel was angry. She expected Lando to restrain his friends who had disrespected her; nonetheless, that was the culture in that low-income neighborhood. People didn't expect women to feel debased when teased - the Feminine Movement idea was too far-fetched then.

Unlike her, Lando didn't pursue a college education. He was content with his high school diploma and making a living as a water carrier for the households in the area. He did not earn enough money because other water carriers provided so much competition that he only worked in the morning. There were a lot of them doing this easy task, which required no experience or college education. In the afternoon, he spent his time hanging around with friends and lolling in the house.

"Why don't you apply for a regular job?" Isabel often asked.

"I do," he would answer. But she knew he didn't. He was too picky and could hardly qualify for the cozy jobs he wanted due to his lack of education and experience. She was just clinging to the faint hope he would see the light and give in to her urgings to join the U.S. Navy. That was the only way she could marry him and live in America, just like her cousin Ditas.

ONE THING SHE AND HIS FRIENDS COULD AGREE ON was that she was very pretty. Ever since she was a child, Isabel often heard the same compliments from her relatives and friends. She was fair-skinned, had mestiza looks, and was quite tall for an average Filipina. Wearing a clean and neatly-pressed dress, no one would believe she lived in a slum area. It was indeed a great equalizer for in the outside world, she even looked prettier than the rich folks who walked around the city.

ISABEL HAILED A PASSING JEEPNEY AND BOARDED. The jeepneys were the mode of transportation in Manila and the suburbs. After World War II in 1945, the American Forces who liberated the Philippines from Japanese occupation left behind a number of surplus war materials when they left for America. Ingenuous Filipino metalworkers converted the army jeeps into passenger jeepneys, which were adorned with two long benches facing each other in the cab and had an entryway in the end. At first they could only

14

sit three to four passengers per row but when used engines from Japan became available, jeepney manufacturers like Sarao and Francisco could build ones that could seat up to 12 people on each side and were sturdy enough for everyday use. The manufacturer gave local artisans a free rein in decorating the jeepneys. The artists painted them in vibrant colors with *sari-manok* artworks that depicted the colorful feathers of roosters on a canvas of gleaming nickel-plated sidings.

Eventually, diesel engines were used due to their economical nature. They enabled the driver to quickly make his "boundary", the amount of money he paid the jeepney owner for the use of the vehicle. The rest of his receipts covered the diesel fuel expenses. Whatever was left would be his earnings. If lucky, he could make up to $7 a day for a 12-hour work; however, this earning was without health insurance, pensions and other benefits as the driver worked on his own. If he was sick, he had no pay. The jeepneys would crawl in the city streets at about 5 miles an hour, stopping to pick up and unload passengers along the way while competing with other vehicles for the limited space on narrow streets. They were often stuck in traffic in ten-minute intervals, especially in the downtown area.

Most of the jeepneys had fragrant Sampaguita flower garlands around the picture of the Virgin Mary or Jesus Christ on the dashboard. The decoration meant that particular driver had paid his daily bribe to the local traffic police. This was a subtle way of operating the illegal activity. The police would use flower vendors to collect the "tong" (bribe), and the drivers paid the vendors the price of the merchandise in addition to the bribe. Before the day started, the police would count the vendors' inventory for the day and get their collection from those that were sold. Many believed the loot surpassed the police superiors and reached up to the highest officials of the city. This was the culture of corruption in a Third World country. Public servants do not necessarily serve the public but also help themselves with the public coffers and, if possible, also with extorted money outside the official budget. In the past, it was a standard, yet illegal, operating procedure for public officials to receive ten-percent commission from every public work project or contract. Presently the rate is said to reach up to 50 percent. The markup is passed on to the taxpayers so the contractors could profit from the job. For this reason, many public officials live in mansions, own several cars and properties, and send their children to exclusive schools on their low salaries.

BUT NOT ISABEL'S FATHER. *Mang* (Mister) Gusting was a rare breed. He was one of the public servants who stuck to their principles and would not accept bribes or do illegal things to augment his measly salary. Some view this as a quixotic quest as most people, when given the opportunity, would enrich themselves. Because he would not do so earlier in his career, his supervisor relegated him to a lowly position so the higher ups would not need him to play along.

"Ayaw kong pakainin ang pamilya ko ng nakaw (I don't want to feed my family with stolen food)," he would tell people.

To stay clean was a tremendous social pressure and caused numerous difficulties. The price of being honest and incorruptible was stiff. He had to endure seeing his family live in squalor in a dilapidated house on a smelly body of water. He witnessed his children's envy of their friends who could afford to buy material goods and enjoy family vacations.

16

Mang Gusting could not be blamed for not trying hard. He used to work a second job as a bookkeeper in a small firm and would routinely go home after midnight and return to work at eight in the morning. The long hours took their toll on his health, and he was advised to take it easy; otherwise, his family would not have a husband and father to provide for them.

Despite this, he made sure his family had the basic necessities. His children wore clean, modest clothes; they ate enough, albeit simple, food; they attended good, though not exclusive, schools; and they received constant parental guidance and supervision during family dinners together and whenever possible. In contrast to other affluent families who had children on drugs, his children were obedient and serious with their studies.

"Whatever we have is enough for us," he would remind his family. "These are God's blessings for which we should be grateful."

3

Trophy Wife

"Para, mama (stop Mister)," Isabel told the jeepney driver when they reached the corner of Quezon Blvd. and Claro M. Recto Avenue. The jeepney was about to turn right on Quezon Blvd. towards downtown Quiapo. Isabel had to walk straight from the intersection to reach her school. She handed a one-peso bill to a passenger seated at the middle of the row who in turn passed it on to the person seated behind the driver. The driver reached back to get the fare and placed the money in a wooden box attached to the dashboard. He then passed the change back which traveled the same way until it reached Isabel.

Walking along the sidewalk, Isabel smelled the mouth-watering aroma of the newly-cooked *chicharon bulaklak* (deep fried pork intestine), a favorite of Filipinos though a high cholesterol snack. It is best eaten when piping hot and dipped in vinegar sauce, the mildly hot oil trickling down the throat as one munches on the delicious morsel. The eatery along that sidewalk served the best chicharon bulaklak in the country. It is called "bulaklak" because once the intestine is fried, it looks like a flower, which in fact is the English translation of its name. On the corner was the Roman Cinerama, the first and only wide-screen theater in the country, which the politically-powerful Roman Family of

Bataan Province owned. For more than a year after its opening, it showed the epic movie, "How the West Was Won."

After reaching Morayta Street, Isabel crossed the street and turned right towards her school.

"BAKIT NANDITO KA (Why are you here)?" Isabel asked her boyfriend Lando who was waiting for her at the school gate when she was done with class at about four in the afternoon.

"Why, don't you want to see me?" he asked, smiling. "I want to take you on a date today."

"My parents will be waiting for me."

"We won't be late."

He held her hands and led her across the street. They went inside the Little Quiapo Restaurant popular for its special *halo-halo* (sweets with shaved ice and milk) topped with ice cream.

"Mukhang kumita ka ng malaki (You seemed to have earned a lot of money)," she told him.

He just smiled. They had a lively talk and she laughed at his jokes as they ate their *halo-halo*. After the meal, Lando looked at the bill and reached for his wallet in his back pocket. He was quiet for a while. Finally, he looked up and asked, "Can you spare some change? My money is short."

Isabel felt insulted and embarrassed. She felt bad because she realized the boy she was dating could not even afford to buy her a snack. When she realized he was serious, she grudgingly took out a ten-peso bill from her wallet.

"Baon ko ito sa limang araw (This is my allowance for five days)," she said without looking at him.

He tried to amuse her as they waited for the waiter to give her the change, but Isabel could not be consoled. Once she got the money, she stood up and hurried outside the restaurant. Lando tried to catch up with her, but she walked fast toward Quezon Blvd. where she would catch her jeepney ride home.

"Wait, I thought we're going to watch a movie?" he asked.

She stopped and with a sharp glaring look at him, asked: "Do you have money?"

He shook his head and said, "Maybe you could advance it. I will pay you back later."

That was the last straw. She turned around and walked faster. As soon as she boarded a jeepney, she saw Lando walking along the side. The jeepney was moving slowly as it picked up other passengers.

"Can't you even pay for my fare back home?" he asked.

She wanted to ignore him but eventually took pity and motioned for him to get inside. She realized she would have no future with her deadbeat boyfriend and resolved to write Ditas, her cousin in the America, to look for a U.S. Navy boyfriend just like what her parents wanted.

ALBERT LOOKED AT HIS WRISTWATCH as he waited for his lawyer in front of the Family Court Building in downtown San Diego, California. After a few more minutes, the lawyer walked out, waiving pieces of papers at him.

"Liberation, baby!" he shouted. He handed the papers to Albert and declared: "You're free!"

Albert was happy. The papers proved that his Mexican ex-wife Teresa had married her boyfriend in Tijuana, Mexico. He, Albert, was no longer obligated to pay her alimony.

TERESA LOOKED LIKE A MOVIE STAR the first time he saw her at a bar in Tijuana three years ago.

"Dito pala sa Mexico, ordinariong tao lang, mukhang artista na sa Pilipinas (Here in Mexico, ordinary people can look like a movie star in the Philippines)," commented Jerry, a friend who accompanied him for a good time in the town across the San Diego border. The movie stars in the Philippines had mestiza looks just like many *senoritas* with Spanish blood and a little of the indigenous Indian lineage in Tijuana.

"Can I buy you a drink?" Albert asked Teresa as he approached her and her two friends.

He was lucky. Teresa could speak English and they could communicate easily.

She smiled. "Yes."

"Si?" he wanted to humor her.

She smiled again.

"Si," she grinned.

21

It was the beginning of their whirlwind courtship. Albert was so engrossed in winning her over he did not think of the consequences of marrying a girl from a different culture.

"Wait till they see my girlfriend now," he told himself as he imagined showing off the beautiful Hispanic girl to his relatives and friends in their Philppine *barrio* (village).

When he was one of the local jobless farm boys with no foreseeable bright future, Albert could hardly get a date among the local girls, who wanted to date only college students from the big city. After joining the U.S. Navy, he had suddenly become a valuable commodity. Girls who used to ignore him were interested, inviting him to their homes when he was on vacation, treating him to a feast. Albert enjoyed watching their mothers butchering the fattest spring chicken for dinner and their fathers taking out their prized possession of *lambanog* (native wine) while they questioned him about life in America. But none of the girls interested him anymore for his standards went up after having a taste of American life. The pretty *barrio* girls whom he had once hopelessly pined as though they were unreachable stars had become uninteresting. Whereas before they saw through him, it was now the reverse – he could now see through them.

Unfortunately Albert was not as wise as he had believed. After he had successfully petitioned Teresa and she had obtained her U.S. permanent resident status, she ceased to be an obedient wife. At one point she would prepare his dinner and clean up after him, much like the ideal wife of his dreams. But Albert found out what a piece of green card could do to his marital life. Suddenly her relatives were staying longer in their apartment. As residents of Tijuana, they had passes that allowed them to come back and forth to the United States. Teresa got a job as a hairstylist and lived an independent life, in particularly when Albert was deployed overseas for six months at a time.

The clash of two cultures, Filipino and Mexican, had taken its toll. He grew weary of the *enchiladas, tacos, burritos* and other Mexican dishes she prepared repeatedly. He longed for the Filipino dishes from his native land that he would always eat as a child. Teresa would not let him cook his favorite *adobo* and *tuyo* (dried fish) due to their stinking up the house. When he brought her to the Philippines, Teresa refused to stay and sleep in their house in the *barrio*.

"It is hot and there are lizards on the ceiling," she complained. The next day, she packed her bags and ordered him to take her to a hotel in the big city.

"May nagawa ba kaming masama sa asawa mo (Did we do something wrong to your wife)?" his mother was worried.

Albert could not give her a satisfactory answer. He was embarrassed before his relatives and friends; however, leaving was a far better alternative than seeing Teresa throw tantrums during their intended two-week stay. He did not even get an opportunity to show off his beautiful wife to his friends and the girls who used to look down on him in the *barrio*.

"Mayroon ho siyang kaibigang Pilipina na asawa din ng U.S. Navy sa San Diego na nagbabakasyon sa Maynila. Gusto niyang makita (She has a Filipina friend who is married to a U.S. Navy serviceman in San Diego and is spending her vacation in Manila. Teresa went to see her)," he explained lamely.

He knew his mother would not buy it, but like any loving mother, her son's interests came first. She pretended to understand her daughter-in-law's disrespectful behavior.

"Kaya pala (I see)," she sadly muttered.

4

Life-Changing Letter

"Inay akina nga ang address ni Ditas (Mom, give me Ditas' address)," Isabel asked, still seething mad. She left her boyfriend Lando as soon as they disembarked from a jeepney at the street corner. Throughout the ride, she stoically stared ahead, trying to control her anger. He knew she could not be appeased and stayed out of her way.

"Mukhang nagbago ang ihip ng hangin, ah (The wind direction seemed to have changed)," her mother commented. "Before I could not convince you to write to your cousin Ditas in the States and look for a U.S. Navy boyfriend for you. Now you are taking the initiative."

Isabel did not respond. She knew her mother was right. Finally, she was convinced Lando would ignore her pleadings that he join the U.S. Navy so they could live in America once they got married. With his nonchalant attitude, plus the fact he could not even afford to treat her to a snack during the supposed date, she knew she could not expect a bright future from him.

"Heto (Here)," her mother handed her a piece of paper. "Make sure you send your best picture, the one taken at Ditas' wedding."

Indeed Isabel looked beautiful in that photo dressed as a bridesmaid. The groom, a U.S. Navy guy, paid for the make-over of everyone in the entourage, especially the girls. This was the first time she wore makeup, and even she had to admit she looked very pretty. The groom surely must have had second thoughts in choosing her cousin Ditas over her. Still, Isabel did not know him as he had grown up with Ditas in the province. The groom did not know the bride had a much prettier cousin until it was too late.

ISABEL SAT DOWN by their dining table and began writing.

"Is this the only copy left?" she asked her mom.

"Of course not," her mother replied. "I had many copies of that photo made. I knew it was a good investment."

It was embarrassing, but her mother was right. Her beauty was their key to a bright future as they could not rely on their father to uplift them from the quagmire of poverty. He was too honest to be corrupt and enrich himself through illegal activities in his government job. He would not even accept small bribes. Her stay-at-home mom could only urge her children to marry well, especially Isabel because her beauty gave her the best chance to attract an affluent suitor.

"Make sure you mail it right away," her mother ordered her. *"Huwag mong i--asa sa kartero* (Don't rely on the postman)."

"I will go to the post office myself before school tomorrow," she promised. For the first time in a long while, Isabel was in full agreement with her mother.

ALBERT'S MISERY WITH HIS MEXICAN WIFE CONTINUED. Teresa had become so independent and indifferent that after only a year, they ceased to treat each other as husband and wife. They still slept together on the same bed but when he woke up early in the morning, she would be fast asleep. When he arrived home, she was still out with friends and Albert would be deep in slumber when she would come home, quietly slipping under the bed sheets.

"Kuwidaw ka sa misis mo, baka gumagawa ng milagro (Be alert with your wife, she might be up to mischief)," a friend once advised him.

He dismissed the warning as he was convinced Teresa, though an uncaring wife, was at least faithful. But he was wrong. One day, while walking towards the beauty shop where she worked, he saw her car parked at the end of the lot. He wanted to surprise her and take her to lunch. As Albert walked towards the car, he noticed there were two people in the front seat, his wife and a man. The two were surprised when he tapped at the glass window.

"Who's that guy?" he asked her.

"Mi amigo, no, mi primo (My friend, no, my cousin)," she answered in Spanish.

It was obvious to the three of them she was lying. Albert could hardly contain his anger. He wanted to smash the glass window and hit her face. But his good nature prevailed upon him, and he instead just sulked away, tightly clenching his fists.

THAT EVENING, he waited for Teresa to come home, ready for a confrontation. She came in just before midnight, and as soon as she saw him, she demanded, "I want a divorce."

He did not reply. He was already dressed up, ready to leave as soon as she arrived. He knew he could not stay in the same house with her that evening. It would be a long night. If he gave into his anger, only God knows what he could have done. Their confrontation might become violent, and he might do things he would eventually regret. Albert instead took the high road, walked out, slammed the door, and drove away in his car.

The long drive in the freeway eased his anger. With the smooth jazz music playing on the radio, he drove all over San Diego until he almost ran out of gas. By that time, he was at peace with himself and accepted his fate. Albert checked in at a motel and tried resting his tired body although he was not able to sleep. At eight in the morning, he informed his office he would not report for work. He went to their apartment and saw Teresa taking out her things with the man from the day before. Albert was not yet in the mood to talk to her and certainly not her boyfriend. As soon as they saw him, he turned around, boarded his car and drove away. He filled his car with gas and drove as far as Los Angeles. In Burbank, he knocked at his cousin's house and told him what happened.

"Mabuti na rin ang nangyari, Kuya (It's good it happened)," his cousin consoled him. "We have long suspected your wife was having an affair, but we could not tell you. It was just a rumor going around among our relatives and friends when one of us saw them together."

As fate would have it, he was the last to know.

THE DIVORCE PROCEEDINGS STARTED QUICKLY. The couple barely had any property to divide between themselves and with no child custody to fight for, the judge granted the divorce. As if to add insult to injury, the man Albert had seen in the car with Teresa accompanied her in the court proceedings. Later, he found out he was Teresa's boyfriend in Tijuana long before the marriage, and why Teresa married Albert when she already had a boyfriend became clear. She wanted to obtain a permanent resident status in America by marrying a U.S. Navy personnel; however, her timing may have been wrong as she was caught too early in the game. Had they stayed together for at least ten years, she would have shared Albert's pension until she remarried. Then again, her sole objective must have been to get her green card, divorce Albert, and marry her boyfriend.

"Remind me," Albert told his friend Alex. "The next time I get married, it must not be with somebody without a green card. I want my next wife to marry me for love, not for the permanent residency status I can provide."

By that time, Isabel's letter to her cousin Ditas seeking a U.S. Navy personnel husband was on its way to America.

5

Last Man On Earth

After just two weeks, Ditas received the letter from her cousin Isabel. Enclosed was a beautiful picture of Isabel taken when she was a bridesmaid in Ditas' wedding. Ditas was surprised. Whenever Isabel's mom would tell her daughter to send a photo to Ditas (so Ditas could find a U.S. resident husband for her), Isabel would not hear of it. Suddenly, the photo and the letter arrived.

Ditas put the photo in her wallet - just in case it came in handy. She had mixed feelings though. While she wanted to help her cousin fulfill her dream of settling in the United States, Ditas doubted whether it was the right way for Isabel to achieve happiness. That was the route Ditas took, but things did not work out the way she hoped.

"DITAS, IPASOK MO NA ANG BAKA sa bakuran (Put the cow inside the backyard)," her mother, *Aling* Lucing, yelled at her from their *batalan* (dirty kitchen).

That was ten years ago. She was twelve years old then, growing up in their province in Bulacan. She was skinny, not because she watched her weight, but because they did not have enough to eat. Her house dress was loose, a hand-me down from her cousin Isabel who lived in the city.

Ditas was barefoot. Her rubber sandals were finally beyond repair, no matter how many times she tried tying the thongs together. Her feet were used to the sharp pebbles and thorny ground thanks to the rough calluses that developed like hard shoe soles. It was already dusk, and darkness was enveloping the area. Before, they used to let their cow graze in the field near their house overnight. But after hard times fell on the area and rustlers came, cows were reined in during the night.

She led the cow in and tied its rope to a tree. Once her younger brother, Berto, made the mistake of tying the rope to a post of their house. When the cow was agitated and went berserk, it pulled away the rope causing the back part of their house to collapse. The cow was their remaining prized possession. They used to have a carabao which their father used to farm the land owned by their landlord from Manila. But since her father died six months ago, they had to sell the carabao to survive. There was no money coming in when their father, the family breadwinner, passed away.

He just came home with a cough that developed into a high fever later that evening. The next morning, he had to return to the farm despite his ailment and help with the harvest, which had to be done right away due to an impending typhoon. It was an unusual situation. Rain was pouring down despite it being almost summertime. After toiling under the hot rays of the sun, his father soaked in the rain to harvest the remaining rice stalks. This was a mistake. Throughout the night, his fever rose so high he was hallucinating. The family could not afford to take him to a doctor and settled with a *herbolario* (quack doctor) who rubbed coconut oil on the patient's back and placed wet leaves on his forehead. Sadly, he did not survive the night. The family was sure he died of something else, but it was too late and too expensive to conduct a post mortem. A coffin

31

was made out of cheap wood. For five days and five nights, his neighbors, friends and relatives stood vigil during the wake to raise money through card games to help the family shoulder their funeral and living expenses. The poor farmer was survived by his wife Lucing, his daughter Ditas, and his two sons, Berto and Mario.

"*Papaano na kayo ngayon, papaano kayo mabubuhay* (How are you now, how can you survive)?" well-meaning friends asked the family. All Lucing, the mother, could do was cry. They learned how to survive as the days went on, but the leftover money from the wake ran out. They started to feel the familiar pain of hunger in their stomachs. This time, the pain persisted as the days without food became frequent. The mother, the daughter and the two boys started going out to the fields, pulling out wild grasses to be sold as horsefeed to *carretela* (horse carriage) operators in the area. When the money coming in was not enough, Lucing did laundry work for rich families in town. Through all these hardships, Ditas managed to continue going to school. Her brothers, who were not studious anyway, dropped out and helped the family make a living.

"*Talbos ng kamote na naman* (Camote leaves again)?" Mario complained one evening as they sat on the floor eating dinner through the flickering light of a gas lamp. "*Hindi na ba tayo kakain ng isda* (Are we not going to eat fish anymore)?"

"*Maghintay ka lang anak. Mag tatag-ulan na, makakakuha na tayo ng dalag, palaka at suso sa pilapil* (Just wait, son. Soon it will be rainy season and we can get mud fish, frogs and shellfoods in the rice fields)," Lucing consoled her son.

"*Binebenta naman ninyo ang mga mahuli namin, eh* (But you sell whatever we catch)," Mario complained.

"*Sus, tama na. Mas kailangan natin ang pera* (Stop it. We need more the money)," Ditas reprimanded her younger brother.

Lucing could not help but cry. She too was tired of eating camote leaves, but they could only afford to survive, not to enjoy life.

"*Hamo, paglaki ko at makapagrabaho na ako, maka-ahon na rin tayo sa kahirapan* (Don't worry, when I grow up and I get a job, we can lift ourselves from poverty)," proclaimed Ditas.

DITAS GRADUATED FROM HIGH SCHOOL years later but could not afford college. She wanted to become a doctor but knew that for her, it was not a dream but a fantasy.

"*Balang araw, makapapapag-aral ka din. May awa ang panginoong Diyos* (You will eventually go back to school. God is merciful)," her mother consoled her.

At seventeen, she was already a grown woman and exuded a simple beauty. A childhood neighbor, Romy, was already courting her; however, he was the farthest thing from her mind. For one thing, she was ambitious and didn't want to remain poor forever. She wanted to work hard first, earn a living, and provide a better life for her mother and brothers. For another, she didn't particulary like Romy. He was an irresponsible kid who hardly went to school, did not work and was always drinking and gambling with friends.

Still Romy persisted on pursuing her, until he became the butt of jokes among his friends.

"Let me make this clear with you again," Ditas once told Romy when he accosted her while tipsy from drinking with friends nearby. "I will never marry you even if you are the last man on earth."

The friends laughed hard and Romy retreated in shame. The next day he left town and she didn't hear from him until she received a letter from the United States Naval Base in San Diego from her jilted suitor, now a member of the U.S. Navy.

6

Her Parents' Daughter

At first Ditas ignored Romy's letters, but they kept coming. He wrote her at least twice a week and people began to notice.

"Wala sigurong magawa ang taong ito (This guy must have nothing else to do)," she told herself.

"Sagutin mo naman, kawawa naman ang tao (At least answer his letter, the guy is pitiful)," her friend Angie said.

"Why don't you answer him yourself," Ditas replied. *"Ikaw ata ang may gusto* (You might be the one who likes him)."

"If he wrote to me, I would," Angie answered. *"Mabilis pa sa kidlat* (As fast as a lightning)."

But Ditas was reminded of her last statement to Romy: "I would never fall for you even if you were the last man on earth."

It was not that she had regrets and wanted to take it back. As far as she was concerned, her main goal was to work hard, save a lot of money, and provide a better life for her mother and two brothers. The last thing she would do was get married and devote her time and energy to a husband and neglect her own family. But out of courtesy, she succumbed to peer pressure and wrote to Romy.

"Kumusta ka na (How are you doing?)" she wrote. "I hope you work hard so you can take care of your family."

This polite response triggered an avalanche of letters. When at first she only got two a week, Romy started flooding her with letters every day. He confessed he had been in love with her since they were kids growing up in their *barrio*. He recalled even trivial incidents about their encounters, which she did not remember. Her attitude toward him remained unchanged. She remembered him as an easy-going guy who liked to hang out and drink with friends. In fact, he barely graduated from high school before joining the U.S. Navy, the last resort for many boys in their neighborhood.

But then her mother got sick.

HER MOTHER'S FRAIL BODY SIMPLY GAVE UP AFTER YEARS OF HARD WORK. She would stay in the field picking wild grass to sell to horse owners. She could be found in the field whenever she was not doing laundry work for rich folks in town. One day in the field, she collapsed. Her family rushed her to the town doctor who advised her to rest.

"Your mother has a weak heart," the doctor told Ditas. "She needs an operation right away."

The prognosis seemed like a death sentence to Ditas' mother. There was no way she could undergo an operation because the family could not afford it. Nonetheless, Ditas sought the help of their relatives and friends, although she knew it was a futile attempt. They were poor themselves and had nothing to spare. She even received a scathing rebuke from her Aunt Marta, her mother's only sister and the mother of her cousin Isabel.

"*Kasi kayo, pinababayaan ninyo ang ina ninyong magtrabaho para sa inyo* (It is because you let your mother work hard for you)," she reprimanded her niece. She didn't even give Ditas fare money to return to the province.

In the end, all she could do was cry and feel helpless.

"*Umutang ka muna kay Romy* (You borrow money from Romy)," Angie suggested when Romy's letter for the day arrived.

Ditas would not hear of it, but then she heard her mother cough inside the room. Her mother was growing weaker every day. Finally, her love for her mother prevailed. She got a ball pen and started writing in a piece of paper. "Dear Romy," she wrote.

The letter merely requested for financial help as she explained her mother's grave situation. "Don't worry, I will pay you back," she promised in the end. "Even if I offer myself in servitude to other people."

It took only one week for Romy to receive her letter and another day for $2,000 to arrive on Ditas' doorsteps. Right away, the heart operation was scheduled. After a month in the hospital, Lucing was back home. But she was not the same as before. The operation merely stopped her from getting worse. She remained frail and weak, unable to do heavy tasks like doing the laundry for rich folks or working in the fields. To top it off, she needed to continuously take her medications, which her family could not afford.

Ditas tried her best to get a decent-paying job, but as a high school graduate, all she received was an offer to work as a saleslady at a department store.

"Isn't it against the law?" she asked Vilma, a family friend who had recommended her for the position. "How come that store can get away paying its employees half of the required minimum wage?"

"*Kaysa naman sa wala* (It is better than nothing)," Vilma explained. "Besides, *nakatayo ka lamang naman maghapon* (You are just standing at the store the whole day)."

Ditas knew at that rate, she would not make ends meet for her family even if she worked two jobs. She was at her wits end when Romy came home for a vacation. At that point, her mother was taking her required medication less often than needed. Ditas was afraid it would take a toll on her.

"*Pasensiya ka na, hindi pa ako nakakabayad sa iyo* (Sorry I still haven't paid what I owe you)," she apologized when Romy appeared at their doorstep. She learned beforehand he was coming.

"*Okay lang iyon* (That's okay)," he replied. "How's your mom?"

She just managed a bitter smile. She was embarrassed to tell him her mother was getting worse for lack of medication and that she needed more help.

Romy could sense her problem. Like a cat that had his prey cornered, he later proposed: "Marry me, Ditas, and I will help you take care of your mom."

She flashed a bitter smile once again as tears started flowing down her eyes. She didn't, couldn't give him an answer. Romy left the house later like a young boy hopelessly in love. He visited her every day until he returned to his work in the U.S.

Days passed but Ditas didn't have time to think about Romy's offer. The pressure from her relatives and friends and her mother's worsening condition forced her to make a rash decision. It was a decision made with her head and not her heart. Growing up she had long fantasized of being financially independent one day, of being able to earn a living, make enough money to buy things she liked and provide for her family.

"Balang araw, makakaraos din tayo sa kahirapan (Someday we will uplift ourselves from poverty)," she kept telling her mother and brothers.

It was at that low point that she missed her departed father.

"Mag-aral kang maige anak, iyan lamang ang maipamamana ko sa iyo (You study hard, daughter. That's the only thing I can bequeath to you)," her father kept saying when he was alive. *"Ipagtataguyod ko ang pag-aaral mong maging doktora habang nabubuhay ako* (I will support your education to become a doctor while I am alive)."

Tragically, he did not live long enough to make good on his promise.

7

Coming to America

All of Ditas' childhood dreams crumbled when she realized she needed more money than what she could possibly make to keep her mother alive. Her mother's continued need for medication required a substantial infusion of money into the family coffers. It was an impossible task with the limited earnings Ditas earned from her job. Her dream of someday making it on her own, making enough money to provide subsistence, if not luxury, to her mother and siblings was now an impossibility. And the only way they could survive, Ditas realized, was to accept Romy's marriage proposal and settle in the United States. In doing so, she would be able to send enough money to her family to ensure the continued supply of medicine for her mother.

Reluctantly, she wrote Romy a letter accepting his marriage proposal. In the letter, she admitted to him that at that time, she did not have any feelings for him. She was doing so in the hopes he could help her with her financial needs, especially her mother's medical expenses.

"I hope that eventually, I will be able to love you and even now, I promise to be a good wife for the rest of our lives," she wrote at the end of the letter.

It was an awkward message, but she felt she needed to be honest from the start. And for Romy, it was good enough. At least he would realize her childhood dream of marrying Ditas, and he was confident she would eventually learn to love him.

Romy sent more money for Ditas's mother's medical expenses and instructed his sister, who was still living in the *barrio*, to make the wedding preparations. Ditas wanted a simple wedding, but Romy insisted on an extravagant affair so he could show to his townmates he made good his brag he would marry Ditas someday.

"Naku Lucing, masuwerte ang anak mo, makakapag-asawa ng U.S. Navy (Your daughter is lucky, Lucing. She will marry a U.S. Navy enlistee)," Ditas' Aunt Marta told her younger sister. "I've been telling my daughter Isabel to look for a U.S. Navy guy to marry, but she insists on that good-for-nothing boyfriend, Lando."

Isabel, who overheard the perennial comment from her mother, made a nasty face. A seamstress was getting her and her bridal entourages' measurements at Romy's expense.

Romy arrived a day before the wedding. On their wedding night, the marriage was consummated inside the only room of Ditas' small house. She had a convenient excuse for showing not much affection. She kept telling her husband to keep quiet as everyone in the house could hear their every movement. Unknown to Romy, when he was already fast asleep, her bride spent the rest of her wedding night quietly weeping.

IT TOOK ONLY A FEW MONTHS for Ditas to arrive in San Diego where Romy was stationed. Romy picked her up at the airport and brought her directly to their apartment. Some of Romy's relatives, including his parents, were there for a *bienvenida* (welcome) party. Later in the evening, when the party was over, Ditas cleaned up the kitchen and retired to their room.

"Why are your parents are still here?" she asked her husband.

"They live here with us," he told Ditas. "They have been with me since they arrived two years ago."

Ditas realized their married life would not only include her and her husband but his parents as well.

LIFE IN AMERICA was not what Ditas had expected. She would rise early in the morning to prepare breakfast for her husband and her in-laws, clean up the house and do the laundry. Her in-laws, on the other hand, spent their time in the mall, the park and senior citizen centers where they would spend their Saturday afternoon dancing. Right away, she realized she needed to get a job to get away from it all and so she could send more money for medical needs and other expenses of her family. The money Romy gave her was not even enough to cover their basic household expenses.

"Sinong mag-aasikaso sa nanay at tatay ko kung magtatrabaho ka (Who will take care of my mother and father if you will work)?" Romy angrily asked her when she informed him of her plan.

"But I need money to send to my mother," she replied.

"Problema ba natin iyon? May kanya-kanya na tayong buhay (Is it our problem? We have our own lives)," Romy told her.

Ditas was shocked. She was sure she made it clear with Romy she would need to help her mother. In just a few months, he already forgot his promise. In contrast, whenever Romy's parents asked money from him to be spent in the casino, Romy's pocket was wide open.

Against her husband's wishes, Ditas quietly asked around for a job. She was just a high school graduate and could not qualify to get a steady job in an office. One of the few options for her was to work at a McDonald's. She wanted to apply as a caregiver because it paid more, but the home care facilities needed a live-in employee, one who could take care of the patients twenty-four hours a day.

"Iyang asawa mo, sandali lang dito sa Amerika, malaki na ang ulo (Your wife, she's just here in America for a few months and she's already getting a big head)," Ditas overheard her mother-in-law tell Romy after discovering Ditas was going to work.

"Bayaan na ninyo siya. Bahala na siya sa buhay niya, hindi ko na siya bibigyan ng pera dahil may trabaho na siya. Simula ngayon, siya na ang bahala sa panggastos natin dito sa bahay. (Let her. I won't give her anymore money since she has a job already. From now on, she will shoulder our household expenses here)," Romy told her mother.

"Eh sino ang mag-aasikaso sa amin (And who will take care of us)?" his mother asked. "Who will do the laundry, clean up the house and cook for us?"

"She will do those chores when she comes home in the evening," Romy replied. "Let me know if she does not."

43

When Romy realized his wife was determined to work and earn her own money, he had no choice but to accept this. He could not afford to lose her because he would lose face among his townmates if she returned to their *barrio* back home.

"Ikaw, sabi ko na sa iyo. Huwag mong dalhin ang babaeng iyan sa Amerika (I told you so. Do not bring that girl here to America)," Romy's mother scolded her son. She did not mind if her daughter-in-law could hear her reprimand. *"Pag may sungay, susuwagin ka na. Pag lumaki na ang pakpak, lilipad na iyan. Pag nasanay na dito sa Amerika iyan, iiwanan ka na* (Once she grew her horn, she would gore you. Once she grew her wings, she will fly away. Once she gets used to life here in America, she will leave you)."

Romy could not talk back to his mother. He turned to his wife instead and angrily told her: *"Nakita mo na ang ginawa mo? Ikaw ang buwisit sa buhay ko* (See what you did? You are the pest in my life)."

Romy went out, slamming the door. As usual, he would spend the night drinking with his friends.

His parents gave Ditas an angry look. She sheepishly retreated to her room and cried.

8

Pretty Girl's Photo

Every day in America was a long day for Ditas. She would wake up at three in the morning, shower and then dress for work. Before four, she would cook breakfast for her husband and his parents and go to work at quarter to five.

The bus ride to McDonald's was at least an hour long and usually more. She helped open the restaurant at 6 a.m. and worked for the next twelve hours.

Ditas wanted to work more hours, preferably until the restaurant closed at 10 p.m., because she needed all the money she could get. Her minimum wage salary was barely enough to cover the household expenses Romy told her to shoulder in exchange for her being allowed to work and able to send the money to cover her mother's medical bills. But her husband insisted she be home at five in the afternoon to cook dinner for him and his parents. He wanted dinner to be ready by the time he got home at six.

After dinner, Ditas would clean up the house and do the laundry. Romy's parents would be busy watching their favorite shows on The Filipino Channel and rarely lifted a finger to help her with the household chores. In their minds, Ditas had to pay back their son Romy's generosity of marrying her so she could come over to the U.S. and get a green card. The green card to them was their own personal property - they alone had the right to bestow it to anyone of their choice.

While Ditas may be their son's preference rather than theirs, they did not want her to get away that easily. And by the time she went to bed, Romy would expect Ditas to fulfill her more physical obligations to him as a wife.

"Asawa na, alila pa (I'm already a wife and also a slave)," she would mutter to herself. Ditas did not complain and instead opted to make the most of the situation. It was her nature to be good and put the interest of others, especially her mother's, before her own.

Her husband Romy also used the situation to his advantage. On weekends, he would be out with friends when he was not dating other women. Ditas learned about his affairs from his friends' teasing him during drinking sprees in their apartment. Romy did not exert any effort to hide his infidelities; rather, he seemed to relish the fact she was aware of his behavior to make her jealous. Although she was his wife, Romy was unsure she loved him despite her diligently fulfilling her marital duties and more.

"Pare, champion iyong bebot na kinuha mo sa Tijuana noong lingo. Naunahan mo lang ako (Pal, the girl you got in Tijuana last Sunday was a champion. You just beat me in picking her)," Ditas overheard Andy tell Romy one time. They were drinking with two other friends, Albert and Ronnie. They were all mates in the Navy.

"Hindi sasama sa iyo iyon, kuripot ka (She won't go with you, you're a cheapskate)," Romy teased Andy.

"Why won't she? She's a sure thing. She's a prostitute," Andy replied. The boys laughed.

46

Any wife would get mad, but not Ditas. She felt relieved her husband Romy was occupied with other things so she could concentrate on her work, household obligations and efforts to send money home. She felt guilty though, because she promised Romy she would try her best to learn to love him. But his errant ways prevented her from doing so. To ease her guilt, Ditas kept praying God for help so that eventually she, her husband and hopefully their future children would become a loving family. When she uttered her marital vows, she was true and sincere. She really promised to love and to cherish her husband until death do them part.

But it was not meant to be. After three years of trying to bear a child, they found out Romy could not father children. His years of patronizing prostitutes took its toll and caused him to acquire a venereal disease, resulting in impotency. Luckily for Ditas, Romy had been cured when they got married and so it was not transmitted to her. But for Romy, however, the damage had been done.

Ditas did not blame her husband. Though she wanted to have children one day, she knew that even if she and Romy could bear one, it would be difficult to take care of a child as her hands were already full with work, taking care of the household and attending to her mother's needs.

The discovery of his ailment led Romy to more drinking sprees with his friends and nights out with prostitutes in Tijuana, Mexico. Tijuana was just fifteen minutes from their apartment in San Diego, California. All one had to do was cross the border and visit the seedy prostitution bars south of the main commercial road, Avenida de la Revolucion.

"Pare, parang mga artista sa atin (Pal, they look like movie actresses in our country)," Andy said, describing the prostitutes to Albert.

Romy was like a young and single Navy recruit on a rest and recreational escapade in the seedy town of Olongapo.

One evening, when Romy and his friends were drinking in the house, Ditas showed Andy the photo of Isabel.

"Check her out, Andy," she told him. "She's looking for a boyfriend here in America."

"No way," Andy replied. "I know what she's up to. She will just marry and leave me once she gets her green card."

"But she's very pretty," Romy told his friend. "With your looks, you can never have a wife as beautiful as her."

As the men laughed, Albert took a look at the photo.

Isabel is indeed pretty, he must admit. So pretty he had to take a second look. And a third. And a fourth.

"Don't tell me you are falling for her," Andy commented when he noticed Albert's reaction. To remind him of what Albert said before, Andy told his friend, "You are the one who vowed not to commit the same mistake when you divorced your Mexican wife. Remember that you vowed to marry a girl who sincerely loves you and not one who is only after a green card?"

Albert could not respond, but the image of the beautiful girl in the picture remained ingrained in his mind.

IT TOOK A WEEK for Albert to give Ditas a call. During that time, he was agonizing over whether to give

Isabel a try. He was fully aware of the bitter lessons he had learned from his ex-wife who just married him to get her green card and eventually married her boyfriend in Tijuana. He knew he might fall for the same trap again. Still, Isabel was so pretty he felt he was falling in love even with her picture.

"What's the address of your cousin Isabel, Ditas?" he called her at work.

"Why, are you interested in her?" Ditas was pleased. Although her experience in America was not as good as she had hoped, she wanted to give her cousin the same opportunity she had. Isabel's experience might be different.

"Yes," Albert admitted. "I will be on vacation next month, and I want to visit her in the Philippines. But don't tell my shipmates about it. They will tease me."

"I understand," Ditas replied. She was fully aware of Albert's experience and his vow to marry only a girl who would love him for who he was, not for his ability to take her to America. In a way, Ditas was pleased because among the friends of her husband Romy, Albert stood out as the most responsible and kindest. She never heard stories about him having a good time with girls and knew she would even envy her cousin Isabel because Albert was the opposite of her husband.

9

The Visit

"*Isabel, Isabel, may sulat kang galing ng Amerika* (You have a letter from the America)," Isabel's mother, Marta, called her daughter as she neared their home. A postman handed it to Marta outside.

It seemed Marta was more than excited to get a letter from the United States. For them, it could only mean somebody had responded to Isabel's request from Ditas that she introduce Isabel to an eligible Navy guy she could marry. That way, Isabel could settle and avail of the opportunities in the U.S.

"*Huwag ho kayong maingay, Nay* (Don't be too loud, Mom)," Isabel cautioned her mother. "*Nakakahiya sa mga kapitbahay* (It is embarrassing to the neighbors)."

"*Hayaan mo sila* (Let them)," Marta dismissed the caution. "*Inggit lang sila kung makarating ka sa wakas sa Amerika* (They will just be jealous if you are finally able to go to America)."

Isabel sat down on a wooden bench inside their house as she opened the letter, her mother right behind. In the letter, Albert introduced himself and told her how Ditas showed them her picture. Albert wrote he would be on vacation in the Philippines in the coming week and would like to meet her.

"*Sagutin mo agad, sabihin mo 'oo'* (Answer him right away, tell him yes)," Marta prodded.

"I can't, it's already too late. He might already be here before my reply reaches San Diego," Isabel answered.

"*Kung ganoon mag-ayos tayo, baka dumating siya kaagad* (Let us get ready then. He might arrive anytime)," Marta said.

THE NEWS OF THE FORTHCOMING VISIT of Isabel's U.S. Navy suitor spread like a wildfire in the neighborhood. Marta could not contain her excitement and even embellished the facts.

"*Guwapo siya at malaki ang suweldo* (He's handsome and his salary is high)," she told a group of nosy neighbors gathered in front of the corner *sari-sari* (variety) store. It didn't matter that she had not yet seen a photo of Albert. The fact that he could take her daughter to live in the U.S. if they got married was good enough.

"*Totoo bang may aakyat ng ligaw sa iyo na galing ng Amerika* (Is it true somebody from America will court you)?" a worried Lando, Isabel's boyfriend, asked the next time he brought her supply of bath water.

"*Oo, totoo. Dahil wala akong maaasahan sa iyo* (Yes it is true because I cannot expect anything good from you)," she replied.

"*Akala ko ba, nagmamahalan tayo* (I thought we are in love)?"

"*Noon iyon. Pero matigas ang ulo mo. Ayaw mong sumunod sa gusto ka na mag-join ka ng U.S. Navy* (That was before. But you are so stubborn you did not follow my request that you join the U.S. Navy)," Isabel told Lando.

"Akala ko nagbibiro ka lang. Okay, mag-jojoin na ako (I thought you were just kidding. Okay, I will join now)."

"It's too late. I already have a suitor who is already settled and making a lot of money."

The problems of the entire world seemed to fall on Lando's shoulders. He could not believe what he just heard.

"But Isabel…" he begged, his voice trailing.

She turned her back on him and walked away. Lando got so mad he lifted the container full of water and threw it down. He was about to wreak havoc in the *batalan* of Isabel's house when Marta appeared by the door and looked at him angrily.

"Ipapupulis kita pag winasak mo ang mga gamit diyan (I will call the police if you destroy the things there)," she warned him.

Lando could not do anything but turn around and run away. He was crying.

"SAAN HO ANG BAHAY NI ISABEL CRUZ (Where is Isabel Cruz's house)?" Albert asked a bystander as he arrived in the neighborhood a week later. The guy pointed at an alley that led to the wooden bridge towards Isabel's house, which sat on top of a body of water.

Lando was nearby, drinking *siyoktong*, a cheap Chinese wine, with his friends as he wallowed in sorrow. Lando could barely look at Albert who neared Isabel's house.

"Upakan natin, gusto mo (Should we beat him up)?" a friend asked Lando. But everyone knew it was easier said than done. The barangay people in the area were so strict they could easily land in jail if they committed mischief. All Lando could do was drink some more.

"Tao po (Hello)," Albert called from outside the house. Isabel appeared at the window and smiled.

She was much prettier in her person than in the picture. He was mesmerized and could not utter a word. Isabel disappeared from the window and reappeared at the door.

"Halika tuloy ka (Come in)," she said. It was as if they did not need to introduce each other. They knew why Albert was there, which made for a somewhat awkward and embarrassing moment.

"Pasensiya ka na at maliit lamang ang bahay namin (Sorry our house is just small)," she apologized.

He just smiled. She pointed at a wooden bench and said, *"Upo ka* (Sit)."

For a few moments, they could hardly look at and talk to each other. The silence was broken by the voice of Isabel's mother as she appeared at the door of an adjoining room.

"Ikaw ba si Albert (Are you Albert)?" Marta asked.

"Opo(Yes)," he shyly replied.

"Buti naman natututuhan mo itong bahay namin (It's good you found our house)," she said again.

"*Idirowing po ni Ditas ang direksyon dito kaya madali kong nakita* (Ditas drew the direction here - that's why I easily found it)," he answered.

"*Dito ka na maghapunan, ipagluluto kita ng sinigang sa bayabas, sabi ni Ditas paborito mo raw iyon* (You will have supper here. I will cook *sinigang* with guava. Ditas told us it is your favorite)."

Albert shyly smiled again. When they were alone, he finally found the courage to talk to Isabel.

ALBERT STAYED IN THE HOUSE until ten o'clock in the evening. He had dinner with the family, although Isabel's father, who later arrived from work, hardly spoke to him. As the night grew later, he got to know Isabel better and he liked what he discovered. He realized he had fallen in love with her despite his vow to never marry a girl who was only after a green card and pass to the U.S. It was obvious to him these were Isabel's intentions, but he did not care. As he left the neighborhood that evening, a group of boys threw a rock at him. They scampered away when he turned around to find the culprit. One was left behind, too drunk to run away. It was Lando, Isabel's ex-boyfriend.

10

Boracay

Albert visited Isabel for the next few days. Every time he came by, the whole neighborhood gawked at him, a U.S. Navy personnel courting and on the verge of marrying their local beauty and bringing her to the United States. It was the dream most people in the area shared. Lando, Isabel's ex-boyfriend, was too heartbroken to witness the unfolding events. He spent his days at home, occasionally stepping out drunk and muttering the name of his lost love.

When Albert felt the heat of the neighborhood eyes ogling each time, he came up with an idea.

"Why don't we spend a vacation in Boracay?" he proposed to Isabel.

Isabel knew it was the best way for them to have privacy and get to know each other.

"I will need my mom's permission," she replied.

"BORACAY? *Maganda daw doon. Hindi pa ako nakakapunta doon eh* (The place is said to be beautiful. I have not yet been there)," Marta blurted when told of Albert's plan. "I hope I can go there someday."

Albert took the hint.

"*Bakit hindi ho kayo sumama, para masaya* (Why don't you join us so it will be more fun)?" he asked. He expected Marta to decline this perfunctory invitation as she knew, or at least should know, the real purpose of the trip was for him and Isabel to get to know each other better.

"*Papaano ang mga bata* (What about the kids)?" Marta asked instead. She was referring to Isabel's younger sister and brother who would be left behind.

Albert had no choice but to say, "*Eh di isama ho natin sila* (We can bring them with us then)."

Isabel felt squeamish as she knew Albert fell into his mother's trap.

"*O, sige, kailan tayo aalis* (Alright then, when are we leaving)?" Marta asked.

"*Bukas ho* (Tomorrow)," Albert replied.

Isabel's dad was too proud to join the sortie. He knew Marta was the one running the show. He also knew what his wife and daughter were up to but could not stop them. He felt helpless. Although he did not like the thought of his daughter getting married this way, he could not do anything for he could not offer a better alternative. Even if he persevered in sending his daughter to college, her future in the Philippines, even as a college graduate, would still be bleak. Her best chance was to go to America. The only way she could do so, whether he liked it or not, was for her to marry Albert, who could help her get a permanent residency status in America. Worse, if he stopped the plan, Isabel might end up with Lando, a good-for-nothing high school drop-out whose only means of living was hauling water in the neighborhood.

"ANG GANDA NG BORACAY (Boracay is beautiful)," Marta muttered to herself as the boat ferrying them from Caticlan Port was about to land at the white beach of Boracay. She could feel the gush of wind on her face and already could smell the good life. She felt she would never have a chance to experience the paradise island if not for Albert. Their family income was barely enough to eke out a living, and so the family never had a vacation in their lives.

Marta, Isabel and the two kids stayed in one room while Albert booked another one for himself. Not that Marta would mind if Isabel and Albert stayed together in one room since she had practically given her daughter to her Filipino-American suitor; however, common decency prevented everyone from even toying with the idea. As soon as they had freshened up, the group strolled along the pathways beside the white beach of Boracay. In any given time of the day, a festive atmosphere permeated in the area. Marta was impressed with the white sands and clear waters of Boracay. She never imagined such a beautiful combination would ever be possible. At the end of the day, Albert asked everyone, including the kids, if they wanted to use the massage services offered by some of the women in the beach.

"Nakakahiya sa iyo, gagastos ka pa (It's embarrassing to you. You will spend money)," Marta told Albert.

"Okay lang ho iyon, five dollars lang ang bawat isa (That's okay, it's only $5 each)," Albert replied.

That her prospective son-in-law would consider insignificant 250 pesos, more than half the minimum wage in the country, assured Marta she had made the right decision in pairing him off with her daughter.

This was the first full-body massage Marta experienced in her poverty-stricken life. She felt like a queen, a rich matron enjoying the luxuries life could offer. A woman rubbing her entire body from head to toe with fragrant oil, her muscles being gently massaged with a calm touch, was beyond her wildest dreams. After a dip in the clear and cool water, the group went back to the hotel to shower. They donned the new clothes Albert had bought for them in one of the stalls. Marta and Isabel were wearing comfortable *mumus*, the kids wore expensive khaki short pants and colorful shirts.

Inside a native restaurant, they had a choice of delicious food. Albert ordered a bowl of *sinigang* soup with fish, huge prawns, oysters and pork *inihaw* (broiled). Marta realized what the beauty of her daughter could provide. It was their key to the good life, and she was grateful that while they were not blessed with wealth, at least God made her daughter beautiful. Her beauty would have a better chance of uplifting their family from the quagmire of poverty than the earnings of her husband, who was so principled and moral than he was unwilling to bend the rules to make extra income from his government job. It was the most enjoyable evening Marta had experienced in her entire life, she reflected while lying on a soft cushion of the hotel's bed, the cold air-conditioned air (her first) permeating inside the hotel room.

The family had a long night sleep, waking up at nine the next morning. After showering, they went down the lobby and found Albert reading a newspaper on a sofa. He had already taken his morning coffee and had earlier strolled along the beach.

"Let's have breakfast," he told his companions as he felt the pangs of hunger in his stomach.

Albert chose the native Filipino breakfast consisting of friend rice, fried egg, *tapa* (dried meat) and *tuyo* (dried salted fish); the others opted for something different, food they never had eaten in their entire life: pancakes and cereal.

"Try the Fruit Loops," Albert suggested to the kids. For Marta and Isabel, he recommended frosted Corn Flakes.

"Don't put sugar in your coffee because your cereal is already too sweet," he advised them. "And don't forget to put chopped bananas in your cereal."

A stranger met them outside the restaurant and offered to take them to the different islands surrounding Boracay.

"You will experience snorkeling and feeding the fish with bread held by your bare hands."

"What's that?" Isabel asked. She had never heard about snorkeling.

"It is going under the water with a clear mask and observing life under the sea."

"Baka malunod ako, hindi ako marunong lumangoy (I might drown, I don't know how to swim)."

"Nakakapit ho kayo sa bangka (You will be holding on to the boat)."

In the end, Isabel, her mom and siblings gave snorkeling a try and enjoyed it.

They spent the rest of the afternoon visiting the butterfly exhibits in one part of the town and lolling on the beach. During the next two days, they enjoyed the pleasures Boracay could offer. The day before their return home, Isabel told her mom: *"Gusto ho ni Albert na mapag-isa kami para makapag-usap kami ng husto* (Albert wants us to be alone by ourselves so we can talk privately).”

“*Sige* (Okay),” Marta gave her permission. “So you can get to know each other.”

“*Umorder lang kayo ng gusto ninyong pagkain sa restaurant sa hotel* (Order any food you want to eat at the hotel restaurant),” Albert told Marta. “*Pirmahan lang ninyo ang resibo at isulat ang numero ng inyong kuwarto* (Just sign the receipt and write the number of your room.)”

But before Isabel could leave, Marta was able to give her a message.

“*Pag gusto ni Albert na magsiping kayo, pumayag ka na, para wala ng kawala* (If Albert wants to sleep with you, you agree so he won’t get away).” It was an awkward matter for a mother and daughter to discuss, but Marta wanted to make sure her daughter would not be stupid enough to miss her chance.

“*Si Inay naman* (How could you?)”, whispered Isabel, still maintaining her pride.

ISABEL AND ALBERT SPENT THE EVENING on another side of the island. They had a romantic dinner at a hotel restaurant and strolled on the beach. Albert brought with him two glasses and a bottle of champagne, which they consumed as they sat on the beach after a stroll. Late in the evening, Albert whispered: “It’s already too late to go back to your mom. Let us just spend the evening here.”

Isabel did not reply, but Albert knew she was too shy to express her agreement. He led her up to her feet. They walked towards a nearby hotel, checked in, and spent their first night together in bed.

"*NAKU, ANONG GINAWA NINYO, saan kayo nagpunta? Bakit hindi kayo umuwi kagabi* (What did you do? Where did you go? Why did you not come home last night)?" Marta was hysterical when the two returned the next day.

They did not expect Marta's reaction.

"*Albert ano ang ginawa mo? Pinagkatiwalaan pa naman kita* (Albert, what did you do? I trusted you)!" Marta interrogated Albert.

Albert had no idea how to respond and kept silent.

"*Kailangan pakasalan mo ang anak ko, kung hindi, ididemanda kita* (You must marry my daughter, otherwise, I will sue you)!"

"*Oho* (Yes)," was all Albert could say.

Isabel stayed in Albert's hotel room when they returned to Manila. The next day, the two of them, along with Marta, went to the City Hall to get married. Till the end, Isabel's dad was too decent not to have any part of it. He just prayed to God his daughter made the right choice.

11

Winners and Losers

"*Maghanda tayo ng engrande pagkasal ninyo sa simbahan. Gawin natin sa malaking hotel* (Let's have a big reception when you get married in the church. We'll have it in a big hotel)," Marta suggested after Isabel and Albert got married at City Hall. They were eating lunch at a Chinese restaurant in Chinatown to celebrate.

"*Huwag na ho, Inay. Nakakahiya sa mga kapitabahay natin* (Let's not do it, Mom. It's embarrassing to our neighbors)," replied Isabel.

"*Bakit ka mahihiya? Iimbitahin nga natin sila para mamantikaan ang mga bibig nila at makatikim silang kumain sa malaking hotel* (Why will you be embarrassed? We will invite them so they will have a taste of food in a big hotel)," the mother said. "*Gusto kong ipamukha sa kanila na finally, nakapag-asawa ka na nang magdadala sa iyo sa Amerika* (I want to show them you finally married somebody who can take you to America)."

It was too late for Marta to take back her words. She regretted reminding them that Isabel married Albert not because she loved him but because she could move to the United States. For Albert, it was a reminder of his vow that the next time he married, he would wed someone who loved him, not someone who is only after a green card. He had a bad experience with his first wife, a Mexican woman who, after getting her green card, divorced him so she could do the same for her secret Mexican boyfriend. But Albert was conscious he was breaking his vow when he married Isabel for he had truly fallen for her.

Between the three of them, they understood why Isabel didn't want a big reception. The whirlwind marriage arrangement was obvious to everyone that having a big party would highlight the fact it was not a marriage based on love but rather convenience. In fact, the couple eventually dispensed with a church wedding. A marriage certificate from the City Hall was enough to support Albert's petition to bring his wife to the United States. It didn't matter that the Church had not blessed the marriage.

The trio went to Isabel's house after lunch where neighbors could sense something big happened. After exiting the taxi on the street corner, Marta haughtily walked towards the alley leading to their house.

"*Nag-asawa na ang anak ko* (My daughter got married)," she could not help but tell the first person she met. The news spread like wildfire in the area. It reached Isabel's ex-boyfriend, Lando hours later, for at that time, he was fast asleep on the floor of his shanty, recovering from yet another all-night drinking spree.

"*Intoy, tulungan mo ang bayaw mo* (Intoy, help your brother-in-law)," Marta told her younger child when he met them by the door. By referring to Albert as her son's brother-in-law, she didn't have to announce her sister got married, although it would take a while for the young boy to comprehend what happened. Albert was busy carrying bags

63

of food they bought from the restaurant which would be used for that evening's dinner.

"*Pahinga muna kayo sa silid* (Take a rest in the room)," Marta told the couple.

But the room was small and had no door. All they could do there was just sit and wait.

"*Dito na lang ho ako sa tabing bintana, masarap ang hangin* (I'll just be here beside the window, the breeze is nice)," Albert replied.

It was a hot afternoon and Albert felt uncomfortable.

"*Isabel, itapat mo ang bentilador sa asawa mo* (Isabel, put the electric fan in front of your husband)," Marta ordered.

It seemed Marta already got used to having Albert as her son-in-law while Isabel still felt awkward with her husband, a relative stranger. Hardly two weeks had passed since Albert first entered her life and now he was her husband. Albert felt the same, although he had long prepared for the day he would finally have Isabel as a wife. The first time her cousin Ditas had showed him Isabel's picture, he could not erase her image from his mind.

"*Maghubad ka muna ng sapatos at polo shirt, para maginhawahan ka* (Remove your shoes and shirt so you will feel comfortable)," she told Albert.

"*Okay lang ako* (I'm okay)," he replied.

Isabel pulled another chair and sat by the window. The two of them remained quiet, looking out and wondering what had just happened.

For Isabel, the thought of her ex-boyfriend Lando lingered in her mind. For the first time, she felt pity for him, now that she had given herself to another man. When Albert arrived, her main focus was to marry him, discarding any thoughts of Lando. Now that she had the time to think about it, she realized how hurt Lando must have been; however she did not regret her decision. She had told Lando on multiple occasions to enlist in the U.S. Navy so they could have a bright future together as husband and wife. But he was not ambitious enough to follow her prodding; with Albert, she saw somebody much more responsible and accomplished.

Albert's thoughts were on the coming days with Isabel. He had no regrets although he did not expect to marry Isabel that quickly and easily. He merely wanted to know her better, but the trap set up by her mom gave him no choice but to marry her.

"Anong iniisip mo (What are you thinking)?" Isabel asked Albert.

"Ikaw (You)."

"Bakit, nagsisisi ka ba (Why, are you having regrets)?"

"Hindi (No)," he replied. He leaned towards her and lovingly kissed her forehead.

Marta smiled when she saw the gesture.

"MARENG MARTA, ANO BA ANG NANGYARE (Marta, what happened)," asked *Aling* Anchang, a nosy neighbor who was standing by the doorsteps.

"Wala naman, nag-asawa lang ang anak ko (Nothing, my daughter just got married), Marta hurriedly went to the door and said.

The neighbor had many other questions so Marta led her away from the house and into the nearby *sari-sari* store where others were hanging out. She didn't want Albert to hear what she would say. With neighbors gathered around her, she embellished Isabel and Albert's love story. She told them the couple had known each other for several years and would always meet outside whenever Albert was spending his vacation in the country.

"You didn't see him here because Isabel didn't want him to come. *Magagalit ang tatay niya pag may lumigaw sa kanya. Gusto muna ng asawa ko na makatapos siya ng pag-aaral* (Her father would get mad if somebody courts her. He wants her to finish her studies first)," Marta told everyone.

"Eh, bakit si Lando, pinatulan ni Isabel (How come Isabel had accepted Lando)?" an inquisitive and doubting neighbor asked.

"Alam naman nating hindi seryoso si Isabel sa kanya. Gusto lamang niyang may maghahatid ng pampaligo niyang tubig pag umaga (We knew Isabel was not serious with him. She just wanted to have somebody bring water she could use for taking a bath in the morning)."

Marta's explanation, that Isabel merely used Lando, did not sit well with the listeners; everyone was aware of the real story behind Isabel's sudden marriage. The explanation in fact made the gossip on the matter juicier, one very much enjoyed by inquiring minds. In the end, Marta got frustrated with unending questions and returned to the house.

"Huh, bahala na nga kayo, kung ano ang isipin ninyo. Basta ang anak ko, makakarating sa Amerika at kukunin kami. Hayaan ko na lang kayong mabulok sa buwisit na lugar na ito (Think what you want to believe. As far as I am concerned, my daughter will go to America and bring us there too. I will let you all rot in this God-forsaken place)," she muttered to herself.

AT SIX O'CLOCK IN THE AFTERNOON, Isabel's dad came home from work.

"Tatay, si Albert po, nagpakasal na po kami (Father, here's Albert, we've been married)," Isabel told her dad as she took his right hand and placed it on her forehead. It was a sign of respect among Filipinos.

"Mano po, Itay (Bless, father)," Albert did the same thing to Isabel's dad.

"Pagpalain nawa kayo ng Diyos (May God bless you)" the father told the children, tears flowing in his eyes. He could not help but feel emotional as he realized he was not able to give his daughter the freedom to marry the man of her choice due to his inability to provide a better future for her.

Upon seeing the tears in her father's eyes, Isabel could not help but be emotional too. She hugged her father and sobbed on his shoulder. The father held her tightly, caressing her back with his right hand.

"Don't worry, things will be alright. Let us just keep praying to God," he said.

"*Huwag ho kayong mag-alala, paliligayahin ko ho ang anak ninyo* (Don't worry, I will make your daughter happy)," Albert assured the father.

The family had a nice dinner together as Marta dominated the conversation. Occasionally, Isabel's father would ask serious but relevant questions which Albert would answer to the father's satisfaction. Isabel's father was convinced Albert was a good man and would fulfill his promise to make Isabel happy.

LONG AFTER ISABEL AND ALBERT HAD GONE BACK to the hotel, Lando woke up inside his shanty in the neighborhood. He learned about Isabel's marriage. He was shocked for a while and remained quiet. Lando then cried and rushed out of the door. In front of Isabel's house, he wailed: "*Isabel, Isabel, huwag mo akong iwan. Mahal kita* (Don't leave me. I love you)."

At that time, Isabel was warmly ensconced in Albert's arm as they lay in bed inside the hotel. They looked forward to a bright future ahead of them.

12

Land of Milk and Honey

That was the last time Isabel set foot in her parent's home. Her parents were worried that Lando, her frustrated drunk ex-boyfriend, might harm her so they decided it would be better he not know her whereabouts.

Albert accompanied Isabel while she secured a Philippine passport and filed the necessary papers for her petition for permanent United States residency. All they had to do now was wait. The embassy representatives assured them the petition would be approved in just a few months since Albert was a U.S. citizen and U.S. Navy personnel.

With nothing else to do before Albert's vacation ended in a week's time, the couple went to the mountain resort of Baguio for their honeymoon. They got to know each other better and were satisfied with their marital decisions.

To avoid Lando, Isabel quit school and stayed with her aunt (Ditas' mother) in the province upon Albert's return to the U.S. He gave his wife a $500 monthly allowance, more than enough to satisfy even her mother's whims.

"Let's go shopping," Marta would declare whenever she visited Isabel. But there were no malls in the province then, and Isabel would end up giving her mother some shopping money for her to use when she returned to Manila.

For the first time in her life, Marta was able to indulge herself in shopping sprees, thanks to her generous U.S. Navy son-in-law.

After just a few months, Isabel's petition was approved.

"You come pick me up, this is the first time I'm travelling," she told her husband on the phone.

"It's easy. It's a direct flight to Los Angeles and once you're there, just follow the line to the immigration counter," he assured her.

"Where will I find for you?"

"Once you get your luggage in the baggage claim area, just walk outside and I will be there waiting for you."

"Do I need to buy a jacket here? I was told it is cold in America."

"The weather here in San Diego is great. You won't perspire. It's only cold during winter, but I will buy a jacket for you here so the quality will be better," Albert replied.

"What *pasalubong* (arrival gift) do you want? You want *bagoong* (anchovies) and dried fish?" she asked.

"Don't. The custom people will just confiscate them. Almost all Filipino food can already be bought here. Just come over. I miss you so much. You owe me a lot of wild nights."

"Tange (Stupid)," she replied and smiled.

When her parents bid her goodbye, her father hugged her and said: "Don't forget to say your prayers and don't worry about us."

"And don't forget to send us dollars," her mother added.

"IS THIS YOUR FIRST TIME RIDING AN AIRPLANE?" her seatmate, a woman in her fifties, asked Isabel.

"How did you know?"

"Because you're holding your bag tightly and you look scared. And also, that huge envelope in plastic bag contains the x-ray film carried by first time immigrants."

Isabel sheepishly smiled.

"I'm Alicia," the woman introduced herself. "You won't need that x-ray film. The immigration people never ask for it."

At first, Isabel was glad Alicia was there to give tips on what to expect in America. Throughout the flight, however, she got bored as the tips became boasts typical among *balikbayans* (Filipino returnees to the country).

"Over there, you will be surprised with the number of items in the groceries. Coffee alone has at least twenty brands."

"The roads are wide and whatever food the rich can eat, so can the poor. Steaks are very common to us."

"We don't need a maid there, everything is done by machine. We wash clothes using the washing machine and dryer. All the houses are carpeted and we use the vacuum cleaner to clean up."

71

"What do you do for a living?" Isabel asked to stop the monotony of information about stateside living the *balikbayan* was boasting.

"Caregiver," the woman answered.

"Hindi ho ba ang caregiver, nagpupunas ng puwet ng mga alaga nilang matatanda (Doesn't a caregiver wipes the ass of their old patients)?"

"Sanayan lamang iyon (It's a matter of getting used to it)."

When Isabel probed further on the woman's job responsibilities, her seatmate lost interest in talking about life in America. Isabel finally got her space and was able to sleep.

WHEN SHE WOKE UP, she heard the pilot announce they were just three hours away from their destination. The stewardesses handed them wet napkins to freshen up and prepare for breakfast. She opened the window beside her and saw the clouds below. It was a fascinating moment, her first time to be literally "above the clouds". She never imagined she would have such an experience, and she had her husband Albert to thank for it. While repeat travelers would feel uncomfortable in the tight space due to the small seat space, the trip was pleasant for Isabel because it was a new and novel experience for her.

LIKE EVERYONE ELSE, she was worried when she lined up before the immigration officer. She had heard horror stories of travelers being denied entry to the U.S. and sent back to the Philippines on the first flight home. Fortunately all of her papers were okay. And just like what Alicia told her, the officer didn't bother to ask about and look at the huge envelope containing x-ray film inside a plastic bag. It was burdensome to carry and identified the new immigrants among the other seasoned travelers.

"Welcome to America," the officer told her as he stamped her passport, barely looking at her.

Isabel could hardly afford to thank him as she hurriedly walked away, lest the officer change his mind and reconsider his decision to allow her to enter the United States.

"Ganito pala dito (So this is how it is)," she muttered to herself as she watched the baggage carousel move and other passengers pick up their respective luggage.

She could still feel the haughty stares of some of the Filipinos around, looking down on her as a newcomer. Her huge x-ray film was a giveaway. Unconsciously, she slowly folded the huge bag into a small piece and placed it under her arms.

As soon as she got her two pieces of luggage, she put them in a cart and followed the other exiting travelers towards the custom inspection and out into the lobby of the airport. She saw Albert right away, waving at her excitedly. She was so relieved that she hugged him and let him kiss her lips.

"Wasn't it easy?" he asked.

"Next time, I want you to be with me. I don't want to be alone," she replied.

"You will never be alone. I will make sure of that."

Isabel felt so grateful she hugged her husband again. Now she felt secure. They walked towards the gate and out into the street. For the first time in her life, she saw America, its clean surroundings, tall buildings and orderly flow of traffic. She felt its cool breeze of air. She was so happy that after a long arduous journey that started when she had first sent her photo to Ditas, her dream of coming to America, the land of milk and honey, was fulfilled, .

13

American Dream

From the lobby of the airport, Albert and Isabel crossed the street into the parking garage. They stopped by a two-seater BMW red sportscar.

"Is this your car?" Isabel asked her husband. "It's beautiful."

"It's a bachelor's car," he replied.

"Maybe you have dated a lot of women with this car."

"No. It was my ex-wife who chose it. When we divorced, this was what I got. I am just a simple guy with simple needs. In fact, I want to replace it with a van."

"Why?" she asked. "A van is too big."

"Won't we need a family vehicle to accommodate our kids?" Albert asked.

Isabel smiled.

"You're rushing things," she said.

"I have to. I'm already old."

"But you're only thirty years old."

"I want to have a lot of kids."

Isabel was pleased with this answer.

ISABEL'S TWO SUITCASES WERE ABLE TO FIT in the trunk of the small car. She noticed a small bag inside.

"What's that for?" she asked.

"Oh, that's my clothing for the next three days. We will stay here in Los Angeles before we go home to San Diego."

"Why?"

"I want to show you around first."

"How far is San Diego?"

"About two hours away."

The two then went inside a nice restaurant for dinner.

"It's expensive here," Isabel commented while looking at the menu. "A meal for one person is already twenty dollars? For that price, you could feed ten people in the Philippines."

"You are already in America," her husband advised her. "Think in terms dollars, not in pesos. Don't convert all your expenses here in pesos. You will just always think everything here is expensive."

Isabel was reminded of the comment of Alicia, who was seated next to her on the plane, that everybody in America could afford to eat steak. She decided to try the dish despite its $30 cost.

"How do you want it done?" the waiter asked her.

She couldn't answer. Finally she asked Albert, "What does he mean?"

Albert smiled.

"Do you want it well-cooked, medium-cooked or rarely-cooked?" he explained to her.

"I'll try medium-cooked."

"She'll have medium rare," Albert told the waiter.

"No, I said medium-cooked," she corrected her husband.

"It's the same. A well-cooked steak is called 'well-done,' a medium-cooked is 'medium rare' and a little bit raw is 'rare'," Albert explained.

"I didn't know there are so many ways to cook a steak."

She blushed. In her mind, she knew she still has a lot of things to learn in living in America.

Albert could not help but smile. He leaned forward and lovingly kissed her forehead. He didn't want her to feel embarrassed.

"All of us pass through that learning process. It's nothing to be ashamed of," he said. "You should see what those from the farms went through."

"There's one guy who made *kalamansi* juice out of the *kalamansi* and hot water given to him by a waiter. He didn't know he was supposed to use it to clean his hands."

"It's such a waste to use *kalamansi* that way," Isabel said innocently.

This time, Albert could not help but laugh. He was just telling Isabel a joke, yet she believed the incident actually happened.

OVER DINNER, Isabel was noticeably conscious of her behavior, which Albert observed.

"Just keep eating. Don't be ashamed. You'll get used to it eventually," her husband advised her.

"I need to buy you a car," Albert said out of the blue.

Isabel could not believe what she heard. She had barely set foot in America, and her husband was already planning to buy her a car. In the Philippines, millions of people had never owned a vehicle in their lives.

"Why? It 's just a waste of money," she said.

"You need a car here. You have to move around. It will take you hours if you use public transportation."

"Does Ditas have a car?"

"No."

"Why not?"

"She needs the money to send to her sick mother."

"How come her husband doesn't buy one for her?"

"I don't know," Albert replied as he broke eye contact with his wife.

He could not tell Isabel that her cousin Ditas was being mistreated by her husband and forced to use her pay for their household expenses while attending to the needs of her selfish in-laws. Whatever was left from her pay as a

78

McDonald's employee was sent to her sick mother in the Philippines.

Vowing not to do the same thing to his wife, Albert told her: "Even if you decide to find a job, I will still give you your allowance and money for our household expenses. Your pay will be yours alone so you can have extra savings."

Isabel was pleased. The parting words of her mother Marta was still ringing in her ears: "Send us dollars right away."

"Just be sexy in the evening," Albert smilingly told his wife.

"I won't have a problem with that," Isabel told herself. She flashed a mischievous smile.

"THAT'S A BIG TIP," she told her husband as she noticed the money he left on the table. "In the Philippines, loose change will do."

"That's in the Philippines. Here you have to give at least 15 percent tip, otherwise, the waiters will give you a dirty look."

From the restaurant, the couple went straight to a nearby hotel.

"I'm tired," Isabel told Albert as they retired to bed.

"I know," Albert told her. "But I'm not."

That evening, Albert collected her long overdue favors from his lovely wife.

IT WAS ALREADY 8 O'CLOCK IN THE MORNING when Albert woke up the next day. His wife was fast asleep. He took a shower and went down to the hotel's restaurant to eat breakfast. Isabel woke up two hours later when Albert was already back in the room.

"Get ready," he told his wife. "I will take you around Los Angeles."

"Mrs. Mendoza, can we clean your room?" a housekeeper asked her as they were about to leave.

Isabel thought she was referring to somebody else but then realized the housekeeper was talking to her. It was the first time Isabel heard somebody called her by Albert's last name. It reminded her once more that the man who was a total stranger to her a few days before they got married was now her husband.

"Yes you may," she answered her with a smile.

THE TRAFFIC IN LOS ANGELES WAS QUITE HEAVY THAT MORNING although they left the hotel way past rush hours. Albert wanted to show his wife around L.A. At the Griffith Observatory, they stood behind the low concrete fence of the parking lot and enjoyed a panoramic view of L.A. Isabel was fascinated. She could see the patterns formed by neatly aligned houses from above. There were no shanties like in the Philippines and everything was clean and orderly.

"Do you know why this place is famous?" Albert asked his wife.

"No."

"This was where the racing scene in the movie 'Rebel Without A Cause' starring James Dean and Natalie Wood was filmed."

"I see," Isabel hardly answered. She had absolutely no idea what he was talking about. Growing up, she had viewed only a limited Tagalog films for lack of movie money and had never seen, more or less heard of, the classic film.

The two then proceeded to downtown L.A. They cruised along Wilshire Blvd., passing in between the tall buildings of downtown up to Beverly Hills. They then turned around and drove along Sunset Blvd. At the historic Grauman's Chinese Theater on Hollywood Blvd., they parked the car and walked along the sidewalk where huge stars bearing the names of famous movie stars were embedded. They boarded a city tour bus and were shown the various tourist spots, including the houses of famous movie stars in Beverly Hills and nearby Bel-Air. Isabel tried to absorb everything although she could not appreciate them at the moment for lack of background information.

"Someday," she told herself. "I will be able to read more about these places and better appreciate my visit here."

The happy couple ate lunch in Chinatown before proceeding to Page Museum at La Brea Tar Pits where they saw the reproduction of tar pits and mammoths during pre-historic times.

At the Queen Mary Museum in Long Beach, California, Isabel had her first experience aboard a cruise ship and enjoyed what she saw. She was impressed and wondered on how the Americans could put together such beautiful places in just one small area in the world.

"I don't think I'll be able to see everything here in America in my lifetime," she told herself.

The thought of bringing her family to the United States, especially her idealistic father, crossed her mind.

"I hope he'll live long enough for me to be able to petition and show him around," she muttered to herself.

She knew her mother would not appreciate much of the beautiful scenery. All that was important to her was to have shopping money. Isabel was also aware she would not have to work hard and make sacrifices to achieve financial gain. She had achieved this security through her husband who already did the hard work and sacrifices for her. And now he was handing her the American Dream on a silver platter.

14

Make Believe World

"Wake up," Albert said as he touched the shoulder of his sleeping wife. "I'll take you to Universal Studios today."

Isabel woke up, a smile on her face. She had a good night sleep, one of the best in a good long time, and remembered what happened last night.

"So this is what marriage is like," she muttered quietly. "Every night….."

"Won't you get tired of me?" she asked her husband.

"Not a beautiful girl like you," Albert kissed her.

Isabel jumped out bed and hugged him.

"What if I am no longer beautiful?" she asked teasingly, nibbling his ear.

"You will always be beautiful in my eyes."

Isabel was grateful Albert came to her life from out of the blue and quite thankful to her cousin Ditas for her role.

"How is Ditas?" she asked Albert.

"You'll see her when we arrive in San Diego in two days. In the meantime, just enjoy 'The City of Angels'."

DITAS WAS HARD AT WORK at McDonald's that very moment. She was a nervous wreck because she had been told the franchise owner wanted to speak with her in the afternoon.

"Did I do anything wrong?" she asked herself.

As far as she could remember, she had been doing the same routine tasks ever since she began working there a year ago. She would arrive at 5:30 in the morning, prepare the food and open the store at 6 a.m. At 5 in the afternoon, Ditas would rush home to prepare dinner for her ungrateful husband and his parents.

Then she thought hard about if she had offended any customers. Did any of them complain to the owner of maltreatment? What if she got fired? How could she find another job? How could she send money to her ailing mother in the Philippines? Ditas would have to stay in the apartment and be at the service of her parents-in-law the whole time. Throughout the day, these thoughts were very bothersome indeed.

ALBERT PARKED HIS CAR at the parking structure of the Universal Studios Theme Park. He and Isabel took the escalator down to the street level. The huge concrete figure of the movie ape, King Kong, greeted them. Neon signs of various stores and restaurants were flashing even though the sun was up. Isabel saw a huge multiplex theater and other signs depicting famous movies along with people walking in every direction.

"Is this Universal Studios?" Isabel asked Albert.

"This is just the Universal Walk. We have to buy tickets to get into the park itself."

"Here alone is already beautiful," Isabel exclaimed.

Albert smiled. He enjoyed showing newcomers like Isabel around and liked seeing their child-like awe and wonder. For him, it was one of the most enjoyable and amusing sights.

Inside the park, they lined up to take the tour. They boarded a tram while a tour guide explained to them everything they saw. They passed by the various sets of famous movies.

"Look, they are going to show us how water was parted in the movie, 'The Ten Commandments'," Albert told Isabel.

Again, Isabel did not appreciate the movie magic for she never had an opportunity to see the classic film.

"Here come the floods," the tour guide exclaimed loudly when they arrived in another set. Water came rushing down from one side and into the street.

"This is how they filmed those flood scenes in the movies," the guide announced.

"Sayang ang tubig (The water is wasted)," Isabel told herself. She remembered how people in their neighborhood, including her ex-boyfriend Lando, would painstakingly pump water from a well and deliver them to various households. *"Dito tinatapon lang sa kalsada* (Here, water is just dumped on the street)."

She didn't know the water was recycled.

85

"Get ready for the earthquake," the tour guide warned when they came to another movie set.

The infrastructure of buildings around them suddenly shook as fires lit up.

"How did they move like that?" she asked Albert referring to the buildings.

"There are mechanisms behind those structures," he explained. He didn't bother to tell his wife there was once a popular film, 'Earthquake', in which the set was used.

The tram then entered a dark sound stage. Suddenly one side lit up and the huge image of a menacing ape leaned forward. It growled, appearing to destroy the structures around it. Isabel was shocked, and Albert had to put his arms around her to calm her down. As one of the highlight attractions at the Universal Studios, the ape was King Kong from the movie of the same name.

They then passed through a movie set depicting a western town, complete with saloons, a bank, horse stable, general store and others. One actor wearing cowboy attire staggered backwards from the flapping saloon doors and fell to the ground in a comical manner. He stood up as another cowboy came out, hit him and he again fell to the ground. The duo then engaged in a fistfight.

"Won't somebody stop them?" Isabel asked Albert in shock.

Albert laughed at the naivety of his wife.

"Don't worry," he assured her. "It was just for a show. They are showing us a typical fight scene in a western movie."

One of the cowboys stood up and ran away. The cowboy who was left behind aimed a gun at him and fired a shot. The other one fell to the ground and the tram moved on to another attraction as the tourists on board clapped their hands.

The set on the movie "Backdraft" depicted buildings burning continuously.

"Buti hindi nauubos ang mga building sa sunog (It's good the fire does not raze the buildings to the ground)?" Isabel asked.

"They're fire-proof and will never burn down," Albert was happy to explain to his wife.

After the tour, Isabel and Albert got off the tram to check out the other shows and exhibits on foot. At a show depicting the movie "Waterworld" starring Kevin Costner, they watched actors re-enact a fight scene in a junkyard scenario. At a movie theater, they watched a short 3-D film that never ceased to amaze Isabel.

"Parang malapit lamang sa akin ang isda (The fish looked like it was right on my face)," Isabel described one particular scene. "I tried to grab it, but I was holding onto nothing."

IT WAS ALMOST 4 O'CLOCK IN THE AFTERNOON. Over at a McDonald's franchise in San Diego, Ditas anxiously awaited her fate. It was a long agonizing wait that was about to end. She saw the franchise owner of the restaurant leave his car in the parking lot. A tall and shrewd Jewish gentlemen known for his no-nonsense business style, he would fire people on the spot even for only minor infractions. This was why he had become a successful businessman, so successful he owned and operated 11 McDonald franchises and 5 Taco Bell outlets in San Diego County alone. As he walked towards the door, he looked grim and pointed out a dirty part of the floor to a McDonald's employee who was sweeping nearby. Ditas had never felt so nervous in her entire life as she awaited her fate.

15

Happiest Place on Earth

Ditas' boss motioned for her to come and sit at a table in the McDonald's where she worked. Ditas put aside the tray she was holding and meekly walked towards him. She was shaky.

"How are you doing?" the owner asked her as they sat across each other.

"I'm fine, sir," she answered.

"You know why I called you up?"

"No sir. Did I do anything wrong?"

"How long have you been working here?" he asked instead of answering her question.

"About a year now."

"During that time, I've watched you work," he said. "I've watched you deal with our customers, relate with your co-workers and do your job."

He paused.

Ditas waited for him to say the word "but" and enumerate the reasons why she would be fired.

"And I am impressed," he said instead. "I have never met a better worker than you."

He continued.

"You are pleasant with the customers and always serve them with a smile. You have worked hard here. I have seen you do other duties not assigned to you, like cleaning up whenever there are no customers. You hardly take any break and you inspire your co-workers to work harder because they would stand out if they took it easy, yet you are friends with them, and I have heard you've even given some of them financial help. You are a wonderful human being, Ditas," the owner finished.

Everything the owner said failed to sink into Ditas' mind immediately. She was still waiting for him to tell her the bad news, but he instead said: "This is why in appreciation for your good work, I am going to promote you to manager."

Ditas could not speak for a moment. When she realized what the owner just said, doubts still clouded her mind.

"But sir," she said. "I am just a high school graduate."

"It does not matter - a college degree is not required for the position. Besides, you are more than qualified because you've already been performing the job for the past months when Merle (the current store manager) was on extended maternity leave."

"What about Merle?" she asked

"She'll keep her job. At least she excelled in something, and that is in hiring you. I will assign you to manage our branch in Chula Vista. I fired its manager a month ago since that store was not performing up to our expectations."

When she realized what had just happened, Ditas broke into tears.

"Why are you crying?" the owner asked surprised.

"Nothing sir, I am just happy," she replied.

At the back of her mind, Ditas remembered all the hard work and sacrifices she made to reach that point in her life: her efforts to help her family, her marriage to a man she did not love, her sacrifices to be a good wife and daughter-in-law despite the maltreatment she had received from her husband and his parents. What the owner did not know was Ditas poured her frustration into her job by doing more than what was expected of her and to temporarily forget her problems in life. She was also glad she was assigned to the Chula Vista outlet, which was just walking distance from their apartment. Now she would not have to take a one-hour early morning bus ride just to reach her work.

The owner stood up and extended his hand.

"Congratulations," he said. "You'll start tomorrow."

He turned around and walked away. And then, he turned back and said: "By the way, your pay will be doubled."

Ditas could not control her happiness. She rushed towards him and hugged her while sobbing: "Thank you, thank you, sir."

The owner smiled and patted her back.

"Just keep up the good work and don't ever change," he said.

Her co-workers sensed something good had just happened. They knew Ditas was expecting the worst, and by the look of things, they believed her talk with the owner ended up much better than expected.

All Ditas was thinking at that moment was the pay raise which she could now send to her ailing mother.

"*MAMAYANG GABI, PAHINGA KAYA MUNA TAYO* (Let's rest tonight)," Isabel told Albert when she woke up.

"*Bakit, nagsasawa ka na ba* (Why, are you getting tired of it)?"

"*Hindi, kaya lang masakit na* (No, but it already hurts)," she shyly responded.

"*Masasanay din iyan, dahil bago pa* (It will eventually get used to it, since it is new)," her husband teased her. "*Ang talagang pahinga niyan, pagdating ng regla mo* (Its real rest will be when your period comes).

She hit Albert with a pillow smiling.

"*O mamayang gabi, game ka ba* (Are you game tonight)?" he teased her again.

She got out of bed blushing.

"*Ikaw ang bahala* (It's up to you)," Isabel softly answered.

She was embarrassed to admit it, but like her husband, she was looking forward to their amourous encounter later that evening.

"LET'S TAKE OUT OUR LUGGAGE. We are checking out now," Albert told Isabel.

They ate their breakfast downstairs, took their showers and were ready to go.

"Why?" Isabel asked.

"We're going to go home to San Diego after we leave Disneyland tonight."

"How long is the drive?"

"Only two hours."

"Ang lapit lang pala (That's close)."

"PUWEDE NA AKONG MAMATAY DITO (I can die here)," exclaimed Isabel upon entering Disneyland.

The sign reading, "The Happiest Place On Earth", loomed overhead. The place was filled with people of different ages, all excited to give the different rides a try.

"Don't die yet," Albert joked. "You still have to see Las Vegas and the Grand Canyon."

Isabel was very happy although she also felt sad. She wished her father, who had sacrificed so much for her, could be there as well. She again wished he would live longer to have the same opportunity to visit the place.

"Let's go here," Albert said as he led her to the enclosed yard next to a hut.

"What's this?" Isabel asked.

"It's the Enchanted Tiki House. You'll be surprised by what you're going to see."

As soon as they were seated inside the hut, the lights turned dark. Lightning flashed, thunder roared and rain poured from outside the closed windows when a spotlight focused on a parrot perched on a stick hanging near the center of the room. To Isabel's surprise, the bird moved and talked in a Mexican accent!

Later, other colorful birds all around the room came to light, talked and even sang to the delight of the audience.

"How did they do that?" Ditas asked Albert when the performance ended. She was holding on to his forearm, occasionally kissing it. She was grateful to Albert for taking her to the park and enjoying a unique experience.

"Through robotics," he answered. "They have mechanisms inside, just like those in robots. You'll see that technology used in many shows here."

They proceeded to the Jungle Cruise, a boat ride along a jungle river bank. Tigers and lions growled at them, giraffes ate leaves off tall trees, a wild boar with long tusks chased a safari guide up a palm tree, and a menacing crocodile scared the passengers until the tour guide shot it. The boat even went behind a waterfall to the delight of the guests. Isabel could not believe what she saw and enjoyed taking everything in.

"Have you seen the Indiana Jones series?" Albert later asked his wife.

"No," she answered.

"What movies have you seen?" Albert asked. He remembered her admitting not to have seen classic movies like 'The Ten Commandments', 'King Kong', and 'Backdraft' while they were at the Universal Studios.

Isabel could not answer.

Then Albert realized his wife grew up poor; watching a movie would have been a luxury for her. He took pity, hugged and kissed her on the forehead.

"Never mind," he said. "You're going to catch up. I am going to take you to a lot of movies from now on."

The thought she had missed out on a lot of fun experiences as a child crossed Isabel's mind.

"HOLD ON," Albert told Isabel once they were seated in a roller coaster inside what looked like a mine shaft. It was dark.

"Don't be afraid, you're with me," Albert said to his wife. Isabel sat closer to her husband, her newly-found security blanket.

The roller coaster moved fast, turned sharply and shot up and down. Along the way, scenes from the Indiana Jones movies flashed on the wall. After the ride, Isabel was very happy.

"I wish I saw that movie," she said.

"Don't worry, we'll rent the entire series and watch them together."

At the Pirates of Caribbean attraction, the line was long but worth the wait. Isabel enjoyed the short cruise in a tunnel aboard a small boat. The sights of the pirates singing, drinking, shooting guns at each other, and their women chasing after them, while animals like pigs and chicken moving like real creatures, amused her. She wondered how she could fully describe what she had just seen to her father so he could have an idea of even half of these wonderful experiences. She was right in aspiring to marry a U.S. Navy personnel after all. In just a few days in America, she had so many fun experiences she could never enjoy in a lifetime in the Philippines.

16

Lucky One

"*Ayoko diyan, natatakot ako* (I don't want to go there, I am afraid)," Isabel said referring to the Haunted Mansion attraction at Disneyland they were about to enter.

"No, it's not scary," her husband Albert assured her. "It's fun."

Still hesitant, Isabel went along with her husband. "We're already here," she thought. She might as well give it a try.

Albert was right. She enjoyed the ride on a two-seater coach that swirled as the ghostly images appeared around them. She did not find them scary, but rather amusing.

From the Haunted Mansion, they walked, passing through the Tom Sawyer Island and Mark Twain Riverboat, Frontierland and the Big Thunder Mountain Railroad. They emerged at the Fantasyland where they rode in a Small World boat. The two entered a theater where they travelled through the scenic spots of America through the magic of movie cameras projected on the surrounding screen. It was a fun afternoon for Isabel and before she knew it, it was already dark.

"Shall we go?" she asked her husband after they had eaten dinner at one of the park's restaurants. She was already sleepy as her body tried to adjust to the sudden change of time from the Philippines to the United States.

"Let's wait a while till ten o'clock," Albert replied. "We'll watch the fireworks."

The fireworks, she had to admit, were worth the wait. It was the first time Isabel had seen such a fantastic display of color in the sky. Mesmerized, she thought she was in a beautiful dream and would never wake up.

"WHERE ARE WE?" she asked her husband when she finally woke up. The sun was up, its bright rays passing through the window. She was in bed, still dressed from the day before, but had a good night sleep.

Albert was smiling.

"You passed out as soon as we left Disneyland last night," he told his wife. "You slept deeply all the way from Orange County to San Diego. I even had to carry you from the car to the bedroom."

"I was tired," she admitted.

She looked around and asked, "So this is your room?"

"Our room," Albert corrected her. "Our love nest."

"It's nice," she said, grudgingly appreciating his joke. It was quite an understatement, for it was a far cry from the rickety floor where she slept on one part of her Manila shanty. She realized that from now on, she would be sleeping in a real bed and inside a bedroom. She stood up and looked out of the window. She saw the other apartments and the main road in front.

"Did you notice anything?" her husband asked her.

"No, what?" she asked in return.

"Our consecutive nightly lovemaking streak was broken. You slept on me last night," he said, teasing her.

"There will be plenty of time for that, don't worry," she teased back. "And now is the time, and we'll do it the rest of our lives."

She went towards her husband, put her hands around his neck, and pulled him down with her on the bed. They made up for what they had failed to do the night before.

'I'M HUNGRY," Isabel whined as she rode on her husband's back as he carried her to the dining room.

It was already 11 o'clock in the morning, too late for breakfast but early for lunch.

To her delighted surprise, Albert had prepared pancakes, bacon and eggs while Isabel had been sleeping. She looked at the breakfast spread on the table as Albert placed her in a chair. There were peaches with cottage cheese, grapes, oranges, apples and orange juice.

She thought of her family back home, who were still contending with *pan de sal* with coconut jam for breakfast. Occasionally, they had fried eggs although her father was happy with a simple meal of dried fish, tomato and fried rice every morning.

"Ang dami naman nito, kaya ba nating ubusin lahat iyan? (This is a lot. Can we eat all of it)?" Isabel asked Albert.

"Of course," Albert was smiling. "I need to eat a lot so I will have the strength and energy to make you happy. *Mahirap nang mapahiya* (It's hard to fall short and disappoint you)."

"You won't," Isabel assured her husband, smiling at his double talk. She was very happy in her new life in America. Everything was turning out much better than what she had expected.

"Where's the hot water?" she asked Albert.

"What do you need it for?"

"I want to make coffee."

Albert led her to the coffee maker and showed her how to brew coffee.

"We don't drink instant coffee here," he told her.

Isabel just had to wait for all the things to unfold before her. She learned how to observe to adjust to the modern ways in America. At first she questioned why Americans needed hot water from the faucet until she realized how convenient and useful it would be.

ALBERT REPORTED FOR WORK LATER IN THE DAY. Alone in the apartment, Isabel unpacked her suitcases and placed her clothes in the drawers and the closets. She lay in bed afterwards, marveling at her good fortune until she fell asleep.

"ATE, ATE (address to an elder sister)," her cousin Ditas was calling her as she shook Isabel's shoulder.

Isabel woke up.

"How did you get here?" she asked Ditas.

Ditas was smiling.

"Albert gave me the key and asked me to bring food."

Isabel hugged her cousin as she regained her composure.

"What time is it?"

"It's eight in the evening."

"Did I really sleep that long?" Isabel asked.

"Yes," Ditas replied. "And you will stay awake tonight. That's what jetlag does to people."

"How are you doing?" Isabel asked Ditas.

"I'm fine," she replied. "Come, let's eat. I prepared *adobo* for you."

"Oh, thank you, thank you. I have not eaten Filipino food since I left Manila. I already miss it."

Ditas set up the table and the cousins feasted.

"You're *adobo* is very good," Isabel was surprised. "I don't remember you being such a good cook back home."

Ditas smiled.

"I used a secret ingredient in this *adobo* recipe," she confessed.

"What?"

"Gourmet vinegar!"

"What's that? I thought vinegar was all the same. *Maasim lahat* (They are all sour)."

"Not this one. It's different."

"Where did you get it?"

"I ordered it from a lady in Seattle."

"How did you know about it?"

"My friend Jesse recommended it. Remember him? The Beatles fan from Manila? He's now in Seattle and we talked one time over the phone."

"Give me some and I will impress Albert."

"So how's your husband? Did I recommend the right guy? Did I disappoint?" Ditas asked coyly.

Isabel hugged her cousin again: "Thank you, thank you very much. *Hulog siya ng langit sa akin* (He's a gift from heaven)."

"How about your husband, Romy?"

"Okay *lang* (He's okay)," Ditas replied, trying to conceal her disappointment and half succeeding.

"How come he's not with you?" Isabel asked, a little curious now.

"He's working overtime," Ditas lied. She knew her husband was out with friends having a good time just like always.

"I thought you were supposed to arrive three days ago?" she asked Isabel to change the topic.

"I did, but we had to stay in Los Angeles so Albert could show me around and take me to Universal Studios and Disneyland."

"Buti ka pa, nakarating ka na ng Disneyland (You're better off since you've been to Disneyland)."

"Why, haven't you been there?" Isabel asked Ditas.

"No."

"How come Romy hasn't taken you there?"

"Kung dito nga sa Sea World at San Diego Zoo, ang lapit-lapit, hindi niya ako madala, doon pa (He can't even take me to Sea World and the San Diego Zoo, which are close)." Ditas replied with bitterness in her voice.

"Why?"

"Because you are lucky, *Ate.* You are lucky," Ditas answered as she hugged her cousin so Isabel could not see the tears flowing down her eyes.

17

Birthday Girl

It took Isabel only a few weeks to adjust to her new life in America. Albert enrolled her in driving school and every day for about two weeks, a Filipina driving instructor would pick her up and give her driving lessons for an hour. She studied for the written test but didn't pass it the first two times. On the third try, she was able to answer the minimum number of required questions correctly. She was not lucky the first time she took the driving test; on the second try, she learned what mistakes to avoid and received her driving permit.

"Driver ka na, puwede mo na akong ipasyal (You're now a driver, you can now drive me around),"* her husband teased her as they left the Department of Motor Vehicles office in Chula Vista on their way to the car.

Isabel was jumping with joy, hopping and skipping towards the car. She knew that a driver's license was the key to being independent in America. Now she could move around and do whatever she pleased. She had her photo taken for her driver's license which would be mailed to their apartment in a few weeks. In the meantime, she was given a temporary driving permit. No more riding buses or jeepneys for her. Isabel had attained the once far-fetched dream from just a few months ago when she was jostling for a seat in overcrowded jeepneys in Manila.

"Can I drive now?" she asked Albert.

He let her.

"You're better off than your cousin Ditas," Albert reminded her. "She doesn't drive at all."

"Yes, why is that?" she asked Albert.

"I don't know," was what Albert could answer. He knew Ditas didn't even have the means to buy a car as all her earnings went to their household expenses and her ailing mother in the Philippines. Romy wanted her to remain dependent on him in moving around so he could keep his hold on her. He spent most of his money having a good time rather than saving to buy a car for his wife. This was a stark contrast to Albert's attitude towards his wife.

THE NEXT WEDNESDAY, Albert went home early and told Isabel to dress up.

"Where are we going?" she asked.

"We'll eat out and celebrate your birthday."

Isabel almost forgot. She's observing her first birthday in America, the first time without her family. Each time, her father would bring home *pancit guisado* (a noodle dish) from a Chinese restaurant in Quiapo and a small cake from a bakery.

"*Pampahaba ng buhay* (For long life)," her father would tell her, subscribing to the common belief that the long noodles extends one's life.

105

This time, however, her father was not around to buy her birthday noodles and cake.

"Daanan natin si Ditas sa trabaho niya at isama natin sa dinner (Let's pick up Ditas in her place of work and take her along for dinner)," Albert told Isabel in the car. "She's your only relative here in America."

But Ditas was not at her place of work.

"She already went home," they were told.

"Let's go home, *bukas na lang tayo mag-celebrate* (Let's just celebrate tomorrow), Albert told his wife.

Isabel was taken aback.

"Nakalabas na tayo, di tayo na lang ang kumain (We're already out, let's just celebrate by ourselves)," she told him.

"No, let's do it tomorrow with Ditas."

"What's the difference?"

"I changed my mind; I don't feel like going out."

Isabel was annoyed and showed her husband her displeasure. Surprisingly, Albert just ignored her change of mood and stuck to his decision to go home.

"This is my worse birthday ever," Isabel pouted, as though she had better birthdays when living in poverty and growing up in a slum.

"Wala tayong kakainin sa bahay, iyon lang tira kagabi (We have nothing to eat at home, just the leftovers from last night)," she told Albert, hoping he would change his mind.

But he did not.

"That's good enough," he said.

Isabel was pissed off but there was nothing she could do. It was the first time her husband Albert did not acquiesce to her wishes. She was surprised at his unusual behavior. He had never been insensitive to her during their few months of living together.

She wondered if he was the real Albert. Perhaps the Albert she knew was too good to be true.

When they arrived home, she noticed a brand new red Honda car parked in front of their apartment. She would have not noticed it if not for the huge red ribbon in front of its hood, but she was too mad to even mention it to Albert. Albert turned the key to their apartment door and let Isabel enter the apartment first. As soon as she was inside, someone turned on the light. She saw a cluster of people inside who shouted, "Surprise!"

And they started singing "Happy Birthday!"

Isabel didn't understand what happened at first until she saw Ditas singing with the group. Then she realized Albert prepared everything beforehand; their planned dinner with Ditas was just a clever ruse.

"Were you surprised, *Ate*?" Ditas hugged and asked her after the singing ended.

Isabel was crying.

"Yes," she replied. "I thought this was my worse birthday ever."

Everyone greeted her a "Happy Birthday" as they introduced themselves. Ditas' husband Romy and his parents were there as well as Albert's small group of close friends.

"Albert asked me to set up everything, including the food. He planned this surprise for you," Ditas told her. "I didn't forget the noodles and cake Uncle used to serve on your birthdays."

Then Albert tapped Isabel on the shoulder and handed her a small red box with a red ribbon.

"Happy Birthday," he said as he kissed her on the lips.

"What's this?" she asked.

"Open it."

She opened the box expecting to see a piece of jewelry in it. Instead, she saw a key. She was confused.

"What's this?" she asked again.

"Look out of the window," he told her.

She looked out and saw again the brand new red Honda car with a red ribbon in front of its hood. Isabel still did not make the connection and looked at him inquisitively.

"That's your car," Albert told her.

When she realized what had just happened, she hugged Albert and cried. She shed tears of joy. Ditas was happy for her cousin but could not contain her jealousy. She had been in America longer than Isabel but still didn't have a driver's license, much less a used car to drive. She looked at her husband who didn't see the contrast between her situation and that of her cousin. A beer in his right hand, Romy was smiling widely as he stood beside his friends and his parents. The contrasting scene didn't escape Albert's attention who took pity on Ditas.

THE NEXT ITEM ON ISABEL'S AGENDA WAS TO FIND A JOB. She sent her resume to different offices with job openings for clerks and secretaries but did not get any response.

"Why don't you work at McDonalds?" Albert finally advised her after her four months of job search. "I am sure Ditas can accommodate you since she's the manager of the store here in Chula Vista."

The thought never crossed Isabel's mind as she fancied herself working in an office. Besides, it was demeaning for her to work with her cousin as her boss.

"I didn't go to America just to work at McDonalds," she replied.

"Why not? How come Ditas is happy to work there?"

"But Ditas is just a high school graduate."

"And you're a college graduate?"

"No, but at least I reached second year in college."

Isabel started getting annoyed.

"You are not supportive of me," she told her husband.

"I am," Albert replied but stopped short of telling her a McDonalds' job pays well, sometimes better than a regular office job, especially if one gets promoted like Ditas. It could be a lucrative career in the long run.

But Isabel had a different idea. She thought she had an advantage over her cousin due to her growing up in the city and Ditas being raised in the province. Of course Isabel was ignoring the fact they had both grown up dirt poor.

18

Bingo!

Six months had passed and Isabel still could not land an office job. It would have been easy for her to simply accept her cousin's Ditas offer for her to work in Mcdonalds, but Isabel would have none of it. She also did not want to hear other people's suggestions of working as a caregiver.

"Jobs are difficult to find here," she complained to Albert one time.

Again, Albert bit his tongue. He wanted to remind her once again she could find a job in an instant if she were not so choosy. But he had learned his lesson. The last time he told her, she gave him a sharp look, cried, rushed to the room and slammed the door. She did not talk to him for days, and he had to contend with preparing his own food.

Eventually, Isabel got tired of looking for a job. She lolled around the house, watched television all day, and sometimes drove around town when her husband was at work. Not that she needed a job. The $1,500 monthly allowance Albert gave her was more than enough to buy their grocery needs with plenty to spare. Albert took care of the other household expenses. Two hundred dollars of the savings was sent to her family back home, and Isabel spent the rest shopping for clothes and other items that caught her fancy.

"Don't send us money anymore," her father wrote to her. "You will need the money more over there especially in time of emergencies."

But before his father's letters could be sent to Isabel, her mother would volunteer to mail them, open them up, read them and throw away any letters advising their daughter to stop sending money. After all, it was Isabel's mother who got most of the largesse. She would spend the money for her shopping needs and eventually as bets in *mahjong* games which, unbeknownst to her husband, she acquired the habit of playing ever since money from the U.S. started arriving.

"Tataba ako dito sa bahay (I am going to get fat here at home)," Isabel muttered as she looked at herself in the mirror. Indeed, she had gained weight for being idle.

"I better get out and get more active."

She joined a nearby sports club and had regular exercises with a trainer. Occasionally, she would pass by Ditas' place of work. Ditas also learned not to give her cousin advice on how to be productive. She didn't want to earn Isabel's ire, which Albert had made the mistake of doing.

One time, Isabel got carried away shopping. The sale at Target was too much for her to handle. Before she knew it, it was almost five o'clock. She would not have time to cook dinner for Albert. The night before, Albert had complained about the fast food dishes she brought home. He wanted her to cook *Tinola* (chicken cooked in ginger soup) for him. Isabel called up Ditas and asked her cousin: *"Anong ulam ang lulutuin mo ngayon* (What dish are you going to cook tonight)?"

111

"I don't know yet," Ditas answered.

"Puwede ba, isahog mo kami at magluto ka ng Tinola (Can you add food for us and cook *Tinola*)?" Isabel requested. "I will pay for it."

"You don't have to pay me," Ditas answered. "Just pass by our apartment at around six and pick up the food."

That gave Isabel extra shopping time. When she arrived at Ditas apartment, she saw Ditas' parents-in-law also coming in.

"Saan ho kayo galing (Where have you been)?" Isabel asked the two.

"Sa iskuwela (From school)," *Mang* Teban, the father-in-law answered smiling.

"You mean you're going to school?" Isabel was surprised. The old man's wife was smiling too.

"Maniwala ka diyan sa Tatang mo. Binibiro ka lang niyan (Don't believe in your Uncle. He's just pulling your leg)," Romy's mother said. "We came from the casino."

"Can you play at the casino during the day?"

"Bukas twenty-four hours iyon (It's open for twenty-four hours)," the old man said. *"Gusto mo sumama ka sa amin bukas, malilibang ka* (If you want, you can come with us tomorrow. You will enjoy it)."

"I do not know the way there. I was told it's far."

"It's easy. The casino bus will pick us up at one o'clock in the afternoon at the parking lot of Von's."

"I will tell Albert about it," Isabel replied.

112

"Don't tell Albert. It might become an issue between the two of you. Just go and come home at about this time; he will not even notice you left the house."

"But I won't have time to cook Albert his dinner."

"What is Ditas for? Just ask her to cook extra food for you."

Ditas chose to be quiet. She did not mind cooking for her cousin; however, she wanted Isabel to steer away from the vice.

THE NEXT DAY, although Isabel thought of joining Ditas' in-laws at the casino, she chose to stay home. However, with nothing else to do, she spent the whole afternoon agonizing over the decision. While contemplating the fact she could have spent the time having fun gambling, the hours at home grew longer and more boring.

"I will give it a try. Just for fun and for one time only," she resolved to herself. "Anyway, Albert will never know."

"What time will you leave home for the bus that will pick you up and take you to the casino?" she asked Ditas' mother-in-law on the phone the next day.

"Twelve-thirty."

"I will pick you up at the apartment. We'll go together to the bus parking lot."

ISABEL WAS SURPRISED TO SEE that the casino was huge.

"*Ang laki pala* (It's big)," she muttered to herself, stepping stepped off of the bus.

"Do you go here every day?" she asked the old couple.

"At one time we could only afford to go here three times a week; now, we're pretty much here every day."

"Where does your gambling money come from?"

Romy's father smiled.

"Don't you know?"

"No," Isabel replied.

"My wife and I receive $600-a-month of supplemental income the government gives to people over 65 years old with no other income."

"That's nice. In the Philippines people with no income will just die away," Isabel observed.

"That's why you and your cousin are lucky for marrying Navy personnel and moving to America. Especially Ditas whom our son Romy picked among his other girlfriends."

"So how can you now afford to go to the casino every day?"

The couple smiled again.

"We hit the jackpot," the old man said.

"Did you win big in gambling?"

"No," this time, it was the old woman who answered.

"Tell her the story, Teban," she ordered her husband.

It turned out that a Filipino man approached the couple two months ago at a weekly seniors dance affair the U.S. government had funded.

"Do you want to earn money?" he asked them.

"Of course," the old man replied.

"Fill out this form and I will give you motorized wheelchairs each for free."

"But we don't need them, we can still move around."

"You don't get the point. I will buy those wheelchairs back from you at $1,000 each, and you'll have extra income."

They were told the government had a program that provided wheelchairs to disabled senior citizens. The man, who sold the wheelchairs and earned large commissions, had an agreement with a Filipino doctor who prescribed the wheelchairs to seniors, even those who didn't need them. The doctor received a share of the commission and the wheel chair company made money out of the products they sold. In addition to his sales commission, the agent would buy the wheelchairs for $1,000 from the recipients who didn't need them and ship them to the Philippines where they could be sold for upwards of $3,000 each. The man shared the earnings with the other members of the syndicate.

"But isn't that illegal?" Isabel asked *Mang* Teban.

"It is illegal if we are caught, but we won't. Everybody is on the take."

"YOU KNOW how to play bingo, right?" the old woman asked Isabel.

"Of course, we play it in the Philippines every time, especially during wakes."

"Here, if you win two consecutive times, you get the $5,000 bonus."

"But that's impossible to do. There are too many competing players."

"That's why nobody has won the bonus ever since we played here."

Isabel gave the game a try. She played five times but did not win and lost $50.

"I am unlucky today, I don't want to play anymore," she said.

"Just one more time, your luck might come," the old woman encouraged her.

And she spoke like a prophet as Isabel won the next game. She was jumping with joy.

"I recovered my capital with profits to boot, I never thought it would be that easy," she exclaimed.

"Let's go home," she told the couple.

"Wait, we haven't won yet. Play more and if you win the next game, you'll get the $5,000 bonus," *Mang* Teban said.

And she did.

19

Lure of the Game

"I won! I won!"

Isabel was jumping with joy. She had just won the bingo game the second time in a row, thereby entitling her to the $5,000 bonus.

"I can't believe it! I can't believe it!" *Mang* Teban was beyond himself. "I've been playing this game for a long time, but I don't remember anyone ever winning the bonus!"

The players around them were also surprised. Here was a girl who played the game the first time ever and right away got the top prize. Indeed, this was a very lucrative beginner's luck, When everything settled down, Isabel collected her prize at the cashier's window. She could hardly count the large stack of $100 bills. Isabel was still euphoric when she put them inside her bag. After a while, she told her companions, "Let's go home."

"Teka muna (Wait)," *Mang* Teban said. *"Mayroon kang nakakalimutan* (You forgot something)."

Isabel checked her bag, looked around. "No, I didn't forget anything."

"Yes, you forgot something," the old man insisted.

"What?" Isabel asked.

"*Iyong balato ko* (My *balato* [money given by a winner])."

"Sorry, I forgot. I was so excited," apologized Isabel.

She took a $50 bill from her bag and handed it to *Mang* Teban.

"What's this?" he asked.

"Your *balato*."

Mang Teban scratched his head.

"*Hija*, you won $5,000. This is too small."

Isabel picked up another $50 and gave it to the old man.

"Give me another $100," the old man insisted.

"But I still have to give others like Albert and Ditas," Isabel explained.

"Forget about them. Don't even tell them we went to the casino and you won so you won't have a problem later on."

Isabel gave *Mang* Teban the additional $100 he wanted.

"How about your *Nana* Munda?" *Mang* Teban pointed at his wife with his pursed lips.

Isabel was forced to get another $200 inside her bag and gave them to the old woman. She was like floating in the air as she walked out of the casino. She could not believe her good fortune. Not only was she able to marry a generous and good navy man who brought her to the United States, assuring her a bright future, but she also won the much-sought after jackpot.

Inside the bus, *Mang* Teban told her: *"Mapapadalas ang punta mo dito sa casino, mayroon ka ng puhunan* (You can now go to the casino often, you already have a capital)."

"I don't know about that," Isabel replied. "Albert might not let me to go."

"Why tell him?" *Mang* Teban said. "He doesn't have to know."

"What if he looks for me during the day?"

"Aren't you looking for a job? Tell your husband you got a part-time job at the casino as a cashier. That way, he won't be suspicious when you're not home."

Isabel was impressed with the creativity of the old man.

"Ang galing ninyo Tatang (You're very good, Uncle)," she told him.

His wife, *Aling* Munda, was beaming with pride.

"Talagang maabilidad iyong Tatang mo (Your Uncle is really creative in making things work)," she said. "He was a fixer in our municipal hall."

Mang Teban was also smiling proudly. He too was impressed with himself.

IT TOOK ISABEL THREE DAYS to find the courage to join *Mang* Teban and *Aling* Munda in returning to the casino. She told Albert she had found a part-time job and was on call. He was pleased that finally his wife would be busy and productive. He knew the pay for such a job would be meager so he didn't bother to ask about the specifics. Anyway, he had told her before that even if she was already

119

earning money, he would continue to give her a $1,500 monthly allowance. Isabel finally was able to have her cake and eat it too, or so she thought. After only playing at the casino for two weeks, she already lost half of her $5,000 winnings. This was because she was not content with playing bingo alone. Isabel learned to bet in high stakes games like *pai gow* poker, black jack and the slot machines.

"I DON'T THINK I'LL BE BACK TOMORROW," she told *Mang* Teban on their way home one time. "I've already lost so much."

"Mababawi mo rin iyon, bubuenasin ka rin sa susunod (You will recover them soon, you will be lucky next time)," *Mang* Teban told her. He didn't tell her he and his wife were already $2,000 in debt at that time. The money they got from the wheel chair scam was all gone, and they were already borrowing money just to be able to gamble.

But Isabel knew better. Coming from a poor family with practically nothing, the loss of the $2,500 was too much for her to forget, even though the money came not from hard work but instead sheer luck in a bingo game,. She stayed home the next few days and told Albert she was not feeling well. Albert told her to see a doctor, secretly hoping she was pregnant with their first child. Isabel did not obey him as she was just faking her ailment, but boredom consumed her while she was at home. She tried to keep herself busy by resuming her shopping sprees and working out harder than ever, but each time, the itch of gambling in the casino bugged her. She wanted to recover the $2,500 she lost and knew she could only do so if she played again. She had to leave.

One day, she could not resist the temptation and showed up at the pickup place for the bus bound for the casino.

"Welcome back," *Mang* Teban greeted her with open arms. At the back of his mind, the old man was gleefully thinking, "I knew you'll be back. You're hooked just like the rest of us."

Isabel won $200 that day.

"Not bad for a day's work," she told herself. In her mind, Ditas would never earn that much despite being engaged in back-breaking work at McDonalds for twice the hours.

Unfortunately, her losses later surpassed her winnings. After another month, she lost the rest of her $5,000 winnings. Isabel was even gambling away her $1,500 allowance. On the third month, she could not even afford the $200 she would send to her mother back home.

"What happened to my money?" her mother called her a week after the money failed to arrive.

"What money?" Isabel asked her.

"The $200 you promised to send to me every month."

"But *Nanay* (mother), I didn't promise to do so every month. They are times when we have money problems as well. What have you been doing to the dollars I sent you?"

Her mother could not answer. She could not tell her daughter she lost the money in the *mahjong* games.

"*Basta magpadala ka lang* (Just send money)," she hanged up the phone right away as she heard her husband about to enter the house from work. She didn't want him to

121

know their daughter had been sending money unbeknownst to her husband and against his wishes.. For Isabel didn't know about her father's advice not to send them money due to her mother intercepting his letters to Isabel and throwing them away.

ISABEL WOKE UP WITH A WEIRD FEELING ONE DAY. She decided not to go to the casino because she thought it might be an unlucky day for her. Besides, she didn't have much money for gambling. Her allowance for the month had already been lost, even though it was only the fifth day. Then the phone rang.

"How was your husband's birthday yesterday?" It was Ditas at the end of the line.

"How did you know it was his birthday?"

"Remember? His birthday is exactly a week after my own birthday. I called him up and greeted him yesterday."

Isabel felt guilty. She totally forgot about it. She was busy gambling she didn't even see her husband that day. He left home while she was still asleep in the morning, and he was already asleep when she arrived at midnight. Isabel had been consumed by a game she had almost won.

"Oh my God, what did I do?" she asked herself.

Right away, she called Albert at work but she was told he was out of the office. She tried his cell phone but there was no answer. She kept calling the whole afternoon but could not get hold of him. At seven in the evening, she started to get worried. Albert would normally arrive home at six and have dinner with or without her. But today, a day after his birthday, he was nowhere to be found.

And then the door bell rang. What she saw when she opened the door shocked her. It would change her life in America forever.

20

Ghost from the Past

Isabel stood frozen. Before her was a person she thought she would never see again the rest of her life: Lando, her ex-boyfriend in Manila whom she dumped for her U.S. Navy suitor and eventual husband.

"Wh-what are you doing here?" she was shaking in fear.

Lando was flashing a mischievous grin. He was like a lion that had cornered his prey.

"I came here to see you," he said smiling. He had a naughty look.

Isabel could not utter a word.

"Won't you let me in?" Lando broke the momentary silence.

"I can't," she managed to say. "My husband is not here."

"What's wrong with that?" he asked. "I am just an old friend. He won't mind."

"He might arrive anytime and get the wrong idea."

"But I just want to talk," he said with a whining pitch in his voice.

"No, I can't," she replied as she closed the door in fear.

"But Isabel, we need to talk," she heard the voice from outside.

"There's nothing to say."

"Isabel!" he called and banged the door.

She remained quiet.

"Isabel!" Lando called and banged the door again. This time, they were louder and Isabel grew concerned with what the neighbors would think.

"Just leave or I'll call the police."

The door banging stopped.

ISABEL ALREADY WAITED FOR AN HOUR but her husband still had not arrived. She was about to call Ditas to keep her company as she was afraid Lando might be lurking outside when she heard the key to the door being turned. It was Albert.

"Where have you been?" she shrieked when he entered. Her pent-up fear was suddenly unleashed.

"I was with my friends," he answered. "They threw me a surprise birthday party at the Officers' Club."

Despite feeling guilty for forgetting his birthday the day before, Isabel was still angry with her husband.

"How come you didn't answer my calls?" she demanded.

"We were in a closed-door meeting the whole day and my cell phone was turned off. I thought you would be at work," he explained.

Isabel's emotions overcame her. She rushed towards Albert and hugged him.

"I waited for you the whole day. I wanted us to celebrate your birthday today. My boss asked me to work overtime yesterday and you were asleep when I arrived," she lied.

"That's alright," he said as he caressed her back.

She felt a sharp object scratching her back and when she pulled away she noticed a bracelet Albert was wearing.

"What's that?" she asked

"Don't you recognize it? It's the gold bracelet you gave me," he answered. "Ditas handed it to me yesterday. She said you had asked her to give it to me as you would be busy at work."

Isabel was momentarily confused. Then she recovered.

"Ah, yes, I forgot," she said.

When she queried Ditas about the gift the next day, her cousin said it was originally her own (Ditas') birthday gift to Albert. But when Ditas realized Isabel might have forgotten about the birthday due to her being at the casino the whole day, Ditas lied to Albert that the gift was from his wife.

"I am sorry, *Ate*," Ditas apologized to Isabel. "I forgot to tell you about it the next day."

"That's alright," Isabel curtly said. "Apology accepted."

She conveniently forgot to refund the cost of the gift to Ditas as she had already lost most of her money at the casino. She didn't even thank Ditas for covering up for her, as if it was Ditas who owed her a favor.

LANDO KEPT CALLING IN THE NEXT FEW DAYS but Isabel would not answer his calls. Whenever she would hear his voice at the other end of the line, she would hang up. One time she disconnected the phone for one whole day, prompting Albert to ask if there was anything wrong with it when he tried calling from his office. When she reconnected the phone, Lando started calling her in the evening while Albert was at home. Lando would hang up whenever Albert would answer his call.

"Somebody is calling here but won't talk to me," Albert told Isabel.

Isabel got worried. She didn't want Albert to know Lando was in the area. He might get jealous and suspect she was reconnecting with her ex-boyfriend.

"Must be a wrong number," Isabel suggested.

When Lando called again while Albert was in the bathroom, Isabel picked up the phone and told him to call in the morning. She wanted to end the calls and thought it would be prudent to talk to Lando and know exactly what he was up to. The next morning, while Albert was at work, Lando called and Isabel asked what he wanted.

"Nothing, I just want to talk to you and see how you're doing."

"I'm fine. You should stop calling me. I'm now married and don't want my husband to get jealous."

"Why would he be jealous? He already won you. I can't change that."

"Then why are you calling me?"

"We've been childhood friends and classmates. What's wrong with saying 'hello' when we're both in this faraway land?"

Isabel calmed down. She realized she might be overreacting and Lando might actually be merely calling as an old friend, not a jealous ex-boyfriend. She thought she should be diplomatic to him so he would not cause any trouble.

"How did you get here?" she asked, her voice calm. She had wondered about it since it was very difficult for everyone, especially with Lando's background and economic status, to get a U.S. visa, even as a tourist. And to do so in such a short time was nearly impossible.

"I applied as a seaman," Lando said. "When our ship docked in Seattle, Washington, I jumped ship and took a Greyhound bus to my friend in Los Angeles."

"Then you have no legal visa?"

"I do now," Lando answered. "My employer had petitioned me."

Isabel wondered how Lando could easily get a job and convince his employer to petition him considering his lack of job experience and high educational attainment.

"What do you do?" she asked him.

"I am an administrator in a law firm."

"How can you become one when you are not a lawyer?"

Isabel thought it would be improbable since she, one who finished second year in college, could not even get a simple office job. How could Lando, only a high school graduate, find an administrator job in the short time he had been in the U.S.

Lando laughed.

"I work for a personal injury lawyer where all I do is refer car accident cases to him. I get a big commission every time. When I found out you are here in San Diego, I asked to be assigned here."

"Why?"

"You are the only person I know from the Philippines, and I thought you might be able to refer people involved in car accidents to me so you can earn big referral fees. By starting with you, I plan to build a wide referral network so I can make big money."

"How did you find me?"

"Your husband is listed in the phone book."

"Now that you have talked to me, please do not call me anymore. I am living a quiet life and don't want any involvement with you and your business. My husband gives me enough money that I don't need your referral fees."

"Enough that you are able to settle your gambling debts?"

"I don't have any gambling debts!" Isabel vehemently denied.

"You will," Lando assured her. "And once you are forced to pay them, you will need me. I have plenty of money."

Then Isabel realized she already lost her allowance money for the month at the casino. She had even used the rent money Albert asked her to give to their landlord. In two days, their landlord would knock at their door and ask for their past due rent payment.

21

Indecent Proposal

Meeting Lando again was like a nightmare Isabel needed. She knew that his arrival in San Diego spelled trouble; however, at that moment, he was the only one who could solve her financial problems. She had gambled away her allowance for the month, even the late rent money her husband had asked her to give to the landlord. Unless she came up with $1,500.00, Albert would discover her gambling problems one way or another.

She waited for one more day, but when she could not raise any money, she had to call Lando.

"You said you can help me," she told him.

"Of course," he said as though he expected the call. "How much do you need?"

"I need at least $1,500.00," she replied.

"I'll drop by your apartment tomorrow at 10 a.m. and give you twice that. You need the extra leg room."

"Not here," she said. "Let's meet at McDonald's in Chula Vista."

Isabel felt safe meeting Lando where her cousin Ditas worked. Even if her husband saw her there, she could claim she was there to visit Ditas and coincidentally had a chance meeting with an old friend. After Lando handed her the money, he then asked her to sign a receipt.

"It's a company policy," he explained. "It's not my money to lend."

He also told her the lender was demanding 20% monthly interest.

"Isn't that too much?" she asked.

"There's no collateral, no credit check, no questions asked," he said. "Where else can you get such a deal?"

The interest might be usurious but Isabel had no choice. She hoped she could use the extra $1,500.00 as capital at the casino, recover her losses and pay her debt. But this was not to be. Isabel suffered even greater losses and incurred more debt from Lando. By the second month, she was $10,000 in debt, with interest running high.

"How can I repay you?" she asked Lando as he loaned her another $2,000.

Lando smiled.

"You will, don't worry," he said enigmatically.

"WE'LL MOVE OUT," Isabel's husband Albert announced one day.

"Why?" she asked.

"I have been transferred to the Naval Base in Norfolk, Virginia," he answered. "We will stay there for the next four years."

"But I like San Diego," Isabel said. "The weather is good, plus I have my cousin Ditas here."

"That's what you signed up for when you married a navy man," Albert said. "You will have to go wherever I am assigned, except when I'm at sea. I know you like your job at the casino, but I am afraid you have to give it up."

Isabel felt guilty. All along, her husband thought she was working part-time as a cashier at the casino. He did not know it was just a ruse Isabel concocted so she could gamble during the day. The move, however, brought forth an interesting dilemma: How she could pay the $12,000 she owed Lando? Isabel spent the rest of the day deliberating what her next step should be.

THE NEXT DAY, SHE TOLD LANDO HER PROBLEM.

"Can I pay you on an installment basis?" she asked him. "At least $500 a month?"

She was thinking of scrimping or even ceasing once and for all the $200 monthly assistance she had been sending to her mother in the Philippines. In fact, since she got hooked on gambling, she had ceased remitting the money, much to the consternation of her mom.

"It will take you forever to repay the $12,000 with that small amount," Lando replied. "My boss will never agree to that."

"How about if I pay you $500 every month?" she asked. She figured she could afford the amount with her $1,500 allowance.

"No way," Lando was firm. "The interest alone is piling up and you cannot pay off the debt with such a minimal payment."

"How about $1,000 every month?" she bargained. Finally, she had accepted the fact that her $1,500 allowance from Albert was too much to spend in just one month. Look at the trouble it got her in.

"No, you must pay the $12,000 before you leave by the end of this week, otherwise, I will tell your husband about your gambling problem and the money you owe."

"He won't believe you."

"I'll show him all the promissory notes you signed."

Isabel was dumbfounded. She realized she was in deep trouble. Albert would find out she was living a lie. There was no job at the casino, she lost all her money in gambling, and perhaps worst of all, she had lied about everything. Albert would doubt her integrity and realize she could not be trusted. There was nobody else she could turn to for help. Ditas was living a hand-to-mouth existence - she couldn't help. Whatever money her cousin made from her job at McDonald's, she spent it on household expenses and the medical needs of her mother back home. Ditas could not even afford to buy new clothes for herself whereas Isabel could shop anytime she wanted when she was not gambling.

"Have pity on me," Isabel begged Lando. "You know I don't have any source of income. I could not pay the money in such a short notice. I was hoping I would win big at the casino and pay all my debts, but it's just not possible now."

Lando flashed a mischievous grin. He manifested the evil look a predator would display at his cornered prey. He let Isabel cry for a while, her desperation becoming more obvious, so she would agree to his demands.

"There is a solution to your problem," he said.

"What?" Isabel asked.

Lando remained quiet for a while.

"What?" Isabel asked again as she looked at him hopefully

He breathed hard and said: "All will be forgiven if you spend an afternoon with me in a motel."

"What?" Isabel was shocked. "No way! My husband will kill me."

"He doesn't have to know," Lando replied.

Isabel was seething with anger.

"Remember, all I have to do is give Albert a call and tell him about your shenanigans."

Isabel felt hopeless. Lando's serious threat was real.

"Why won't you do it?" Lando asked her. "It's only a one-time deal. After that, I'm gone forever in your life. All your debts will be forgiven and you can start fresh in Virginia or wherever it is you're moving. And you'll do so with a clean slate. It's not like we haven't done this before. You were my girlfriend, remember?"

Still, the thought of cheating on her husband Albert never crossed her mind. She may not have loved him when they first got married, but she had learned to do so due to his kindness and generosity. How could she do this to him?

Then tears started to flow in Isabel's eyes. She felt helpless and miserable. There was no way out.

"C'mon," Lando prodded her.

"Why do you have to ruin my life?" Isabel asked. "Why do you want me to get into trouble?"

"You won't," he said. "He will never know. It'll be just between the two of us."

"Can you just forgive me? Can you just allow me to pay my debt on an installment basis? I will pay $1,000-a-month as long as it takes to pay everything including the interest."

"You don't understand," Lando said. "I don't need the money. I have plenty of that. All I need is closure. When Albert came to your life, you just left me hanging in the air. As if I were a disposable item with no feelings."

"And now going to bed with you will bring closure?"

"Yes. That way, I won't feel sorry for myself the rest of my life. I could then finally move on"

Isabel stood up and walked towards her car. She didn't give him an answer.

22

Set Up

That evening, Isabel seemed unusually cold and distant when she and Albert made love.

"What's wrong?" he asked afterwards.

"Nothing," she replied. "There are just a lot of things on my mind."

"What?" he asked. "You're worried about our move to Virginia? You'll going to enjoy it there. While San Diego may have the best weather, you'll experience all four seasons in the East Coast. They're each wonderful in their own ways – it'll be a wonderful experience. Besides, we'll just be there for four years and then move on."

But Albert was not aware of his wife's dilemma.

"Why must we leave so soon?"

"I have one month to report to my job in Norfolk," Albert explained. "But we have to leave by Friday so we can take a road trip across America. I would like you to see Las Vegas, the Grand Canyon and other sights. We'll pass through different states like Arizona, New Mexico, Texas, Arkansas, Tennessee, North Carolina and Virginia. There is so much to see in the U.S., and I can't wait to show you"

To anyone, it would have been an exciting prospect. Seeing a huge part of America, especially to one who was relatively new to the country, should have been a big deal. A rare and lucky experience indeed! But not to Isabel. She had her problems with Lando to contend.

"Will that take a month?"

"We'll take our time. We'll stop in any place to explore it for days if we feel like doing so."

"Why can't we just fly a few days before you report for work?" Isabel was hoping to buy time and somehow raise money to cover her debt.

"No, I want to take this trip with you. We'll remember it the rest of our lives. It's certainly a once-in-a-lifetime opportunity. Besides, we have to bring my car to Virginia."

"What about my car?"

"We'll have it shipped with the rest of our clothes."

"The furniture and the appliances? We need time to pack them."

"Don't you know? This apartment is fully furnished. The furniture and appliances are not ours. I like it that way so we can easily move to wherever I might be assigned next. Trust me, it's a lot less stressful this way."

Isabel ran out of reasons to convince her husband to postpone their trip. At the start, she made up her mind to reject Lando's request to be with him in a sleazy motel and cheat on her honorable husband.

"I would never do that," she told herself.

But hours passed and she could not think of any solution. It was a Wednesday and she only had one day left to solve her predicament before the move. She and Albert had packed most of their things, the rest to be shipped to Virginia. But she realized there was really no way she could raise the $12,000 she owed Lando in such a short time.

"Just one time only," she could recall Lando telling her about his indecent proposal. "After that, you're debt-free, you can start a new life in Virginia, have a clean slate."

"What if Albert finds out?" she remembered asking.

"He will never know. Nobody will know. It's just between the two of us."

Isabel was sitting on a sofa, staring at a blank wall of their apartment, still thinking over the conversation.

"It's not like we did not do it before. You were my girlfriend, remember?"

"I won't, I won't, I won't!" she told herself loudly and stood up.

Then the wall clock chimed. Another hour had passed in what felt like minutes and Isabel was still without a solution to her problem. No matter how much she tried to think of one, she realized she had no option but to accede to Lando's demand. Otherwise, her husband Albert will know about her gambling problem and get mad. He might not trust her anymore and even leave her. The same result that might occur if he found out she cheated on him. What would happen to her then? Would she return to Manila in disgrace? That would be unacceptable.

"At least if I sleep with Lando, there's a chance Albert would not know and I can start a new life," she thought. "If I don't, Albert will surely learn about my gambling and leave me anyway."

"I have no other option but to do it," she convinced herself.

Most important of all, she did not want to ruin Albert's perception of her. It was her desire to keep a clean image, which was now tempting her to ruin her character. It was like her moral father accepting her materialistic mother just to keep their family together.

The decision to give in to Lando's demand would also bring closure to her ex-boyfriend for the hurtful things she did to him, such as unceremoniously dumping him as soon as Albert came into the picture. She did not even tell him she would do so but rather ignored him like he never existed, like they never had a long-time relationship since high school. She treated him like a disposable item, not as a person with feelings.

"Walang utang na hindi pinagbabayaran (There's no debt that is never paid)" was the lesson her father always told his children. And this was her payback for the wrongs she had committed against Lando. The payback, she thought, would be harmless as long as her husband would never know. It would be a secret she would take to her grave. Isabel would finally get rid of Lando, and she would never have to see him again the rest of her life; instead, she could look forward to a long and happy life with her beloved Albert.

During this moment of weakness and vulnerability, she lifted up the phone and dialed Lando's number.

"Meet me at Motor Inn Motel on the corner of Elm Street and Broadway in Chula Vista," he told her. "I'll see you soon."

"ARE YOU SURE ALBERT WILL NEVER FIND OUT?" Isabel asked as Lando led her inside a ground floor room of the motel.

"Of course," Lando answered. "This is just between the two of us."

"How will I know all my debts will be forgiven?"

Lando gave her all the twelve promissory notes she signed, totaling $12,000.

"After we finish, I will sign and write 'paid' in all of them."

But still, Isabel was shaking in fear. She desperately wanted to back out. But ironically, she knew that at that moment, the only way she could stay married to Albert was by cheating on him. She went toward the bed, laid down and covered her closed eyes with her right arm. She hated the moment and wanted to finish it as soon as possible. She wanted her freedom back, a second chance in life. Isabel kept reminding herself she would attain them in just a few short hours, after Lando had satisfied his carnal desires.

Then she heard him say, "Wait here. I'll buy some beer first."

He went out of the room and walked a short distance. He then pulled out his cell phone and dialed Albert's number.

"Hello?" Albert answered. He was at his desk finishing up some paperwork.

"Hello?" Albert asked again after a moment had passed.

The he heard a stranger's voice.

"Is this Albert?" Lando asked, making sure it was Isabel's husband on the other end of the phone.

"Yes,"

"Albert Mendoza?"

"Yes."

"Your wife Isabel is with a man in Room 106 of the Motor Inn Motel on the corner of Elm and Broadway in Chula Vista."

Albert was shocked.

"Hello?" he called angrily. "*Sino 'to* (Who is this)?"

The caller hanged up.

Albert could not believe what he heard. He had never suspected his wife Isabel doing anything wrong. She was at work at the casino during the day and the two would spend their evenings cuddling in front of the television and eventually retiring to bed as lovers. She would never betray him like the stranger claimed.

LANDO PUT BACK HIS CELL PHONE INSIDE HIS POCKET and walked toward the room. He was smiling as he entered it and saw Isabel still lying in bed with her right arm across her closed eyes. He walked towards her. She did not notice he had left the door of the motel room slightly ajar.

ALBERT SAT IN HIS CHAIR FOR A LONG WHILE and thought about this bizarre conversation.

"No way," he kept telling himself. But the more he thought about it, the more he was convinced he could not simply dismiss it. There must be a reason why the stranger took the trouble of relaying the message. Albert stood up and told one of his co-workers he would step out for a while. Knowing the location of the motel, he got inside his car and drove towards it. It was just a ten-minute drive.

His heart beat faster when he saw Isabel's car in the parking lot in front of Room 106, the room number the caller had mentioned. He walked towards the door and saw it was slightly open. Albert called out softly, heard nothing, and pushed the door open. He saw the bare back of a man who didn't bother to look back, as if he was expecting Albert to enter. Then Albert saw the woman lying under the man suddenly rose. She had a surprised look on her face. It was his wife, Isabel.

23

Road to Nowhere

"Albert!" shouted Isabel.

She was shocked to see her husband at the door of the motel room. He was staring at her with a pained expression.

She had been lying in bed, barely lifting her head while Lando was lying naked, face down, on top of her. It was the worse scene a husband could ever imagine. Albert could not stand the sight. His instinct was to move forward and beat up if not kill the two, but he had the good sense to turn around and walk away. For Isabel, it was the worse reaction her husband could give. She wanted him to beat her to a pulp for her transgression and treachery. She wanted him to savor the satisfaction of getting even. She even wanted to be killed as she could not bear the unbearable shame she felt. Albert was the best husband a woman could have asked for: loving, generous and kind. He pampered her with his love and money, providing her with a generous allowance despite her being so choosy in getting a job. Any husband would have complained when she insisted on an office job while other works like those at the McDonalds were available. But not Albert. He allowed his wife to enjoy a care-free life, which she abused and led her to this ugly scene. What had she done?

For Isabel, the pained look on Albert's face would forever be etched in her memory. It was worse than death, one that would haunt her for the rest of her life. When she came to her senses, she pushed away the naked man on top of her. She stood up, grabbed her clothing and put them on. Lando laid on his back with his arms folded behind his head. He was trying but failing to hide the mischievous grin on his face. Everything had gone according to his plan.

With her clothes on, Isabel ran out of the room and called for Albert. She saw his car driving out of the parking lot into the street. Dismayed, she went back to the room crestfallen.

"I am sorry," Lando lied. "I don't know how he found out about us."

"This is all your fault," she railed at him. "Because of you, I betrayed the man I love. I may have lost my good life because of your selfishness. How could you do this to me!"

"Isabel, I swear didn't know this would happen," he lied. "I just wanted closure, remember?"

"Closure *mo ang putang ina mo* (Closure your son of a bitch)," she angrily snapped at him.

Isabel rushed out of the door and boarded her car. Maybe she could still fix things with Albert.

Meanwhile, Lando was left smiling with satisfaction. Everything had worked out perfectly.

Isabel drove her car with no clear destination in mind. So was Albert. He drove straight as fast as he could. He wanted to get away as far as possible, as though a lethal radiation was coming out of the motel room and would catch him if he moved too slowly. He could not imagine his wife Isabel cheating on him, and yet she had.

"What have I done to deserve this?" he asked himself.

He gave her everything she wanted, more money than she could spend. They did not have any relationship problems, at least any that came to mind. Unlike other couples, they barely ever fought because he was always patient with her. What kind of a person could do this to a good and generous man like him? What else could she ask for, as she was living a pampered American Dream life? What Albert didn't know was that it was her lethal gambling addiction that entrapped Isabel into the devious hands of her cunning ex-boyfriend. Ironically, her infidelity was meant to preserve her marriage and keep the love of her husband. It was supposed to be the first and last time, a one-time deal, so she could enjoy a good life with Albert and together they would live happily ever after. It was her fear of losing his love that led her to opt for a risky solution to her problem; of course, Albert did not know any of this. He did not know anything at this point. Like the gambler that she was, Isabel had made a high risk bet and lost. Big time. But Albert was not aware of his wife's dilemma and had no explanation for her errant behavior, except perhaps pure carnal desires and affections for her lover. Or maybe she was simply an evil person.

The treachery brought back the bitter memories of his divorce from his first wife, Teresa. She was a Mexican who, like Isabel, married him for the green card he could provide and the permanent stay in the Land of Milk and Honey, the United States of America. Like Isabel, Teresa also cheated on him after she obtained her green card. She was able to petition her Mexican boyfriend so she herself could give him the privilege to stay in the U.S. for good as a resident alien.

"When will I learn my lesson?" Albert agonized.

He remembered vowing never to marry a girl again without a green card or a U.S. citizenship. He did not want his next wife to use him as a doormat in entering the United States, just like what Teresa did to him. Yet, he fell for the same trap. He had given up this vow and threw caution to the wind when he succumbed to the charms of Isabel, a slum girl who desperately needed to be lifted from the quagmire of poverty she was doomed to live the rest of her life. Why had he done this to himself?

WITH TEARS IN HIS EYES, Albert drove farther and farther like he was escaping a plague. Then he saw the road sign towards Las Vegas and again felt the pain in his heart. Tomorrow, he was supposed to leave San Diego with Isabel heading toward his new job assignment in Norfolk, Virginia. He was looking forward to showing her the glitter of the Sin City, the magnificence of the Grand Canyon, the beauty of the different states they would drive through for a month on their way to their new home in the East. Instead, he was driving alone, the bitter memory of his wife's treachery piercing his heart painfully. He decided to prematurely embark on his journey to the East Coast as the thought of going back to his apartment in San Diego would be too painful. He did not want to see Isabel or anything associated with her, lest he might do something drastic he would forever regret.

He thought he would just ask his friend Romy to pick up all his belongings from his apartment and ship them out to his new place in Virginia. For now, he didn't want to see

Isabel, perhaps for the rest of his life. It was already dark when he passed through the glittery lights of Las Vegas. He pushed on until he got tired and sleepy. At midnight, he stopped by a small motel along an isolated road and checked in. He laid on the bed but could not sleep. He went to the motel's office and rang the bell, waking up the night clerk.

"Do you have any beer?" he asked.

"No," the sleepy clerk responded. "But I have a half finished bottle of whiskey."

"Do you have more?"

"I have an unopened one I intend to drink afterwards."

"Can I have both of them?"

He did not wait for his answer as he handed the clerk a $50 bill.

"Keep the change,"

The clerk happily gave him both bottles.

"Enjoy," he said with a smile.

INSIDE THE ROOM, Albert drank the whiskey until they were gone. He wanted to dull the pain in his heart, erase the bitter memory of what he had just seen. He collapsed in bed drunk, the only time he could enjoy a moment of peace. He would forget about his troubles while he was asleep, yet he knew they would haunt him again when he woke up later. But for the time being, he was at peace.

24

Salt and Water

"Papaano na ako ngayon (What will I do now)?" rued Isabel, crying all night.

She had just committed the biggest mistake of her life, driving away the man she truly loved, one who showered her with material wealth, comfort and sincere affection. Earlier that evening, she went home confused and saw the packed luggage they were supposed to take to their cross-country trip the next day. They were supposed to enjoy the next few days – and the rest of their lives. They would have been the happiest days of their lives, a third honeymoon after their first in the mountain resort of Baguio and their second in the world-famous theme parks in Los Angeles. Now the beautiful dream they weaved just a few days ago crumbled like a castle in the sand. And she had no one to blame but herself.

She waited and waited for her lover to come home, although in her heart she did not expect him to do so after the hurtful betrayal she made him suffer.

She took a shower, trying to get rid of any traces of the man who had dishonored her husband from her body. She must have showered ten times that evening, but the feeling of dirt and shame had remained ingrained. She realized she could only get rid of them if Albert could somehow forgive her, and they could start fresh all over again.

"Ipaligo mo lang iyan (Just take a bath)," she remembered a story about the virtues of the old days when a woman kissed by a man would have to marry the violator, lest she suffered shame from the eyes of the community the rest of her life. Some would advise the girls to 'just take a bath' still, the truly virtuous could not lose the ignominy they felt. Later on, girls could sleep with men with their virtue still intact. But Isabel's case was different from the liberalized norms of modern-day society. She was a married woman who had betrayed her husband. No amount of showering could ever erase her disgrace.

She fell asleep crying in bed. The marks of her dried up tears were visible on the white bed sheet when she woke up later the next day. It was already ten in the morning and the sun was up. She looked around, searching for traces of Albert. She felt the sheet on his side of the bed. It was cold and still neatly spread; Albert clearly did not come home last night. She picked up her tired body, went out of the room and sat on a chair by the dining table. She rested her head on her hand with her elbow on the table. She bowed and closed her eyes. She didn't know what to do. She was transfixed like a stone statue when the ringing of the phone broke the quiet stillness in the house.

"Kailangan mo ba ang tulong, Ate (Do you need help)?" it was her cousin Ditas at the other end of the line. She was not aware of what happened. "I took the day off so I can help you pack and give you and Albert a proper send-off."

Isabel burst into tears.

"Come over, I need you," was all Isabel could say.

IT TOOK AN HOUR for Ditas to arrive at Isabel's apartment. Although Ditas had been in America much longer than her cousin, her husband had not taught her to drive or buy a car like Albert did for his wife.

Ditas was shocked when she found out what happened. She knew her cousin was quite liberated but did not expect her to go to that extreme. Ditas felt guilty. After all, it was she who paired Albert off with Isabel so that her cousin could come over and live in America like her. Ditas knew that Albert had been burned once and had vowed not to marry a girl who needed a green card. She pitied Albert more than Isabel.

"He will be back. He's just letting her hurt feelings subside," was all Ditas could tell Isabel.

But days passed and there was no trace of Albert in sight.

"*SABI KO NA NGA BA MASAMANG BABAE IYANG PINSAN MO, EH* (I knew your cousin is a bad woman)," her father-in-law, *Mang* Teban proclaimed. "*Talagang masama ang lahi ninyo. Kung bakit dinala-dala pa kayo ng mga asawa ninyo dito sa Amerika. Dapat nabulok na kayo sa Pilipinas* (Your family is really bad. Your husbands should have not brought you here in America. You should have rotten in the Philippines)."

Ditas was hurt by what her father-in-law had said. She had just told Romy what happened with Albert and Isabel in the presence of her in-laws.

She remained quiet. She was waiting for her husband to reprimand his father for these hurtful comments. Instead, Romy added fuel to the fire by commenting: "*Sabi ko na nga ba diyan kay Albert, huwag patulan iyang pinsan mo. Pakawala iyang babaeng iyan* (I told Albert not to marry your cousin. She's a loose woman)."

Ditas burst into tears and ran inside her room.

"Naku, nagdrama pa (She acted dramatically)," Ditas overheard her mother-in-law say.

She laid face down on the bed crying. She was hurt by what she heard but not necessarily surprised. No matter how much she tried to respect her husband and his parents, she could not help but feel bad. They had absolutely no respect for her; they did not care if they hurt her feelings. She tried to obey her father's teaching to respect her elders, but at that moment she wanted to talk back and defend the honor of her family. They may be poor but they have dignity; instead, the best she could do was bite her tongue and drown in her sorrows.

AFTER AN HOUR, ROMY'S MOTHER SAID: *"Ano ba? Hindi ba lalabas ng kuwarto iyang asawa mo? Aba, nagugutom na tayo ah* (Won't your wife come out of the room? We are already hungry)."

Just like what she did every day, Ditas was supposed to cook dinner for her husband and his parents. But that night, she felt so hurt that she remained inside the room.

"Tawagin mo na, at utusan mong magluto (Call her and order her to cook)."

Romy stood up from watching TV on the sofa and walked towards their room. He tried to open the door but it was locked.

"Ditas, magluto ka na. Gutom na kami (Ditas, you cook now, we are already hungry)," he said as he knocked at the door.

There was no answer.

"Ditas!" he yelled at his wife.

Still Ditas remained quiet.

"Aba, lumalaki na ang sungay ng asawa mo (The horns of your wife are growing)," *Mang* Teban prodded his son. *"Kung ako, tatamaan sa akin iyan* (For me, I would hit her)."

"Ditas!" Romy was now embarrassed. *"Buksan mo ang pinto* (Open the door)."

Ditas did not respond.

"Ditas!" Romy yelled again. This time, it was louder. He was already raging mad.

When he realized his wife would not follow his demand, he kicked the door open. He saw Ditas lying face down in bed and still crying.

"Ano ba? Hindi mo ba narinig ang utos ko (Didn't you hear my order)?"

Ditas remained silent. She wanted him to apologize; instead, Romy grabbed her by the right shoulder and violently pulled her up so she could face him.

"Susunod ka ba o hindi? Tatamaan ka sa akin (Are you going to follow or not? I am going to hit you)."

Ditas burst into tears. She pitied herself for the disrespect of her husband. She instantly felt all the humiliations she had been suffering during their time together

153

in America. She thought she could withstand all the hardships so long as she could work in America and send money for the medical needs of her ailing mother. But now her husband and his parents, these monsters had crossed the line. There was a limit to a person's sufferings. Ditas had to maintain her dignity for it was her family's honor that was assailed.

Her lack of response drove her husband into frenzy. She remained like a statue, unmoving and unresponsive. To elicit the response he wanted from her, Romy slapped Ditas on the face. Blood flowed from her mouth. Instinctively Ditas covered her face with her hands. But her husband hit her again on the side of her forehead, leaving an obvious black mark. Ditas stood up and ran towards the door. Romy remained in the bedroom catching his breath, out of shape from his late night debaucheries. He was so mad. His parents sneered at their daughter-in-law as she ran past them.

"Tamo, di nakatikim siya. Susunod din pala (See she got what she deserved. She'll obey in the end), *Mang* Teban told his wife.

"Tawagin mo kami pag nakaluto ka na (Call us when you are done cooking)," *Aling* Munda ordered her daughter-in-law as she went inside their room with her husband.

But instead of proceeding to the kitchen, Ditas walked towards the phone and called the police.

FIFTEEN MINUTES HAD PASSED when Romy heard a loud knock.

"Dinner must be ready," he thought as he stood up from the bed and walked toward the door. Instead, he saw several large police officers staring at him.

"Are you Romy?" one of the officers asked him.

"Yes," he answered timidly.

"Did you hit your wife?"

"She was stubborn, she pissed me off," he replied.

"Did you hit your wife?" the officer asked him again, louder this time.

"Yes," he admitted. He could not deny his offense since the mark on Ditas' face was obvious.

"Sir, you are under arrest for assault," the officer said, reading him his rights while his partner handcuffed Romy's hands at his back.

Romy's parents heard the commotion and went out of their room. They also thought dinner was ready.

"What happened?" the father asked.

Romy did not respond as he was being led out of the house.

"How about our dinner? We are already hungry," the mother asked her son like an idiot.

Romy got enraged with the lack of concern of his parents. He railed: *"Putang na* (Son of a bitch). Cook rice and eat it with salt and water. They're always the food you fed us when we were kids, anyway."

And for the first time since they arrived in America, Romy's parents had a taste of the kind of food they used to eat when they were living poor in the Philippines. And this did not make them happy at all.

25

$5,000 Windfall

Romy spent an unpleasant night in jail for domestic violence. He was released the next day because his wife did not press charges. But not after getting a stern warning from the judge.

"Here in America," the woman judge told him, "we honor and respect our women. They are our mothers, our sisters, our wives. They are on equal footing with men and should even be placed on a higher pedestal to be revered. They should not be taken advantaged of and abused."

In addition to the scolding, the judge ordered Romy to attend anger management classes for six months. Any violation of the conditions of his release, according to her, would be met with drastic consequences, which included a blot on his military record that could jeopardize his benefits. Romy was so afraid with losing these benefits that he swore both to the judge and himself that he would never harm his wife or any woman again. He had learned his lesson. Ditas, instead of taking advantage of the situation, meekly continued her role as a dutiful wife and daughter–in–law, doing household chores, cleaning up and cooking dinner for her husband and his parents. Though kind and forgiving, she knew her rights as an American resident. She knew domestic abuse was an abhorable offense that must not be tolerated and must be reported to the authorities. And now Romy knew this too.

ALBERT CONTINUED HIS SNAIL'S PACE DRIVE to the East Coast. He could hardly gain ground as he continued to drown away his sorrows with liquor upon checking in different motels each night. He would drink through the night and wake up at around 10 a.m. the next day. Then he would move on, only to stop and continue drinking at yet another strange, depressing motel late in the evening.

On his sixth day, he looked at the mirror and didn't like what he saw. He saw a disheveled bum, with messy hair, days-old beard and glassy eyes. His skin had broken out, his weight low, his shoulders hunched over, dark circles under eyes. He did not recognize himself: the clean shaven, strong and responsible naval officer of whom hundreds of enlisted men depended. Where was this man now? And of all this because of a girl, a lying cheat. Albert realized he was not solving his problem, but only aggravating it. He began to truly focus his attentions on Isabel and instead of pitying himself, Albert began faulting her; it is she who should be suffering for he was the victim. He pulled himself together, shaved, showered and combed his hair. Still wearing his old clothes, he went out to buy new ones, put one set on, and followed the discipline he had learned in the military. He would act like an officer and a gentleman and would not let marital woes break him down; as a soldier, people depended on his strength. In no time, he reached his destination, reported for duty and moved on.

ISABEL WAS IN AGONY. She didn't know what to do, how she could survive without her husband. Her

157

apartment was in disarray and her appearance messy. Any time, she was expecting a knock at the door. It would be the apartment manager, telling her the check she issued for the rent bounced. But days had passed and the manager never came. She called her bank and inquired about her balance. She was surprised to learn there was $600 left and the rent check she issued was paid. It turned out that the automatic deposit of her $1,500 allowance from Albert on the first day of the month had not been terminated. She was relieved that she wouldn't be homeless despite still carrying a heavy burden in her heart.

"HELP ME," she kept asking her cousin Ditas.

"Pray *Ate*," Ditas would console her. *"Magnovena ka sa Ina Ng Laging Saklolo. Lagi niyang ibinibigay ang bawat hilingin ko. May awa ang Diyos* (Offer a novena to the Mother of Perpetual Help. She always gives whatever I asked. God has pity)."

For the first time in many years, Isabel returned to her faith. She offered a novena and heard mass everyday. She vowed to change her ways. She even became a devotee of the Virgin Mary.

"Can you hire me in your restaurant?" Isabel asked her cousin Ditas.

Ditas was hesitant because she knew her cousin was picky and possibly not trustworthy.

"Any job," Isabel insisted.

She wanted to be useful. She could also use the money. The $1,500 allowance she got was not enough considering she was living in an apartment. She could not move to a cheaper place because she hoped Albert would come home any day. Isabel was also worried the allowance might be cut off eventually. Worse, divorce papers might come. She needed to stand on her own. The sooner, the better.

"*Eh Ate,* we have an entry level position open where you'll need to clean the toilet," Ditas replied.

"It's okay."

With the help of Ditas (being the manager of the McDonald's outlet certainly had its benefits), Isabel got the job. And she proved herself equal to the task by working hard and being appreciated by her co-workers.

A FEW WEEKS AFTER THE MOTEL INCIDENT, two of Albert's friends, Alex and Andy came to his apartment.

"Albert wants us to ship his things to Virginia," they told Isabel.

At least five pieces of luggage containing Albert's belongings had been sitting in the living room since his abrupt departure. They were supposed to be shipped together with Isabel's things after the couple was supposed to leave for the cross-country trip. But the motel incident aborted the plan.

"Where is he? How can I get hold of him?" Isabel eagerly asked the two.

"He does not want us to tell you," was all they could say.

Isabel realized no matter how much he tried, the duo would not betray the confidence of their friend. She could see the ugly contempt in their eyes. She understood their anger since she had betrayed their close friend. She was like a candle melting in shame before them. She went inside her room and cried. When she heard the front door closed, she sobbed in despair. She knew the pieces of luggage would be the last things connected to Albert's presence in the apartment, perhaps in her life. Now they were gone for good. And soon, if not already, would Albert.

A MONTH HAD PASSED and Isabel still could not get hold of her husband. Perhaps it was over.

"His anger is too much and I cannot blame him," she told herself.

She had not lost hope, however. Having become more religious in recent weeks, she prayed every day she would be forgiven and Albert would love her again.

"When that time comes, it will be different. I will be the one serving him, not the other way around."

Her photos with Albert were everywhere in the apartment to remind her of the good times they had together and to inspire her not to lose hope and to focus on her goal of getting him back.

A WEEK AFTER THE MOTEL INCIDENT, Lando, Isabel's ex-boyfriend and cause of her break-up with Albert, started calling her again.

"Your husband is gone. He already left you. You should forget him," he told her. "I will take care of you. I have plenty of money for you to gamble every day."

But Isabel refused to be seduced. The thought of being with Lando made her sick to the stomach. She could not understand how she could have ever been close with him. She saw how lowly Lando's life and character were compared to Albert's, the good and noble husband she drove away. Her knight in shining armor. She was truly in love with Albert and only now did she realize it.

"OPEN THE DOOR," Lando, at one time told Isabel over the phone.

"Why?" she asked.

"Just open it."

"I don't want to, you might enter my apartment."

"No, I am across the street."

Isabel peaked through the hole on the door and saw nobody at the other side. She slowly opened the door and saw a thick envelope on the ground. She picked it up and saw a stack of dollar bills inside in different denominations.

"That's five thousand dollars," she heard Lando say through the phone she was holding close to her ear. "For your gambling money."

"No, I don't want this. Take it back."

"But it's yours."

"I...don't want anything from you. Just leave me alone"

"I want to come over. Let's talk."

"No, don't."

"I will come over anyway, whether you like it or not."

"I will call the police," Isabel warned him.

Lando hung up.

Isabel wondered why the mere mention of the police would shut Lando up. The same thing happened when he attempted to reach her before.

"He might have a problem with the police," she wondered.

The next day, she placed the $5,000 in the collection box of a church.

26

Scam

"*Gusto ninyo ho bang kumita ng pera* (Do you want to make money)?" the voice at the other end of the line sounded familiar to *Mang* Teban, Romy's father.

"*Sino 'to*, Berto (Who is this, Berto)?" asked *Mang* Teban.

Berto was the Filipino guy who had arranged for *Mang* Teban and his wife to get motorized wheelchairs through their Social Security benefits. Since they didn't actually need those wheelchairs but were prescribed to them through the connivance of a Filipino physician, they sold them to Berto who shipped them to the Philippines.

"It's good you haven't forgotten me," Berto laughed as he talked.

"How can I forget you? You're manna from heaven. What will be our money-making scheme this time?"

"Let me come over. We'll discuss the details."

BERTO'S plan was to arrange a fake accident with *Mang* Teban and his wife *Aling* Munda as passengers in a car.

"Isn't it illegal? We might get caught."

"That's why it's called 'easy money', it's illegal."

"We might get hurt."

"You won't. We'll just claim you're inside the car, but actually you'll be outside when our accomplice deliberately rear-ends it."

"Delikado ata iyan (It might be dangerous)."

"You and your wife will get $3,000 each, $6,000 in all."

"Sige, basta ganyang halaga, walang deli-delikado (Okay, with that amount, nothing is dangerous)."

THE FAKE ACCIDENT WAS ARRANGED three days later. The head of the syndicate was somebody who they did not know, though he was familiar to a person they did know.

"Taga saan ka (Where are you from)?" *Mang* Teban asked, trying to break the ice.

"Gagalangin, Tondo," he answered.

"I know somebody from there," the old man said. "Do you know Isabel Mendoza?"

The guy just smiled and said nothing. Of course he knew her. He was Lando, the ex-boyfriend of Isabel. But he just ignored the question.

"Okay, here's the plan," Lando told everybody. "We will go to an isolated area in Otay Mesa. With nobody there to be witnesses, the second car will rear-end the first car which will be stopped on a corner. The driver and the passengers will then go inside the first car. We will call the

164

police and once they arrive, you will all pretend you are hurt. We will use the police report to file a claim against the insurance of the second car. All of you will take physical therapy sessions for one month. Afterwards, we will collect money for damages."

"What if the doctor notices that we were not actually hurt?"

"He won't. There is no way any doctor could ever contradict you as long as you insist you are hurt. Besides, the doctor is one of us. He gets one-third of the claim, my office gets one-third and you get what's left," Lando explained.

"It's easy," *Mang* Teban said smiling. *"Matutupad na din ang pangarap kong maging artista, katambal ko pa ang aking* leading lady (My ambition to be an actor will be fulfilled with my leading lady as my partner)."

He then winked at his wife who approvingly smiled at him.

The fake accident was staged in no time. When the police came, *Mang* Teban and his wife *Aling* Munda gave a performance worthy of an Academy Award.

"I can't move," *Mang* Teban complained dramatically. "My neck hurts."

The paramedics put a neck brace on him, placed him on a stretcher and into an ambulance. He, his wife, and the drivers of both cars were brought to the nearest hospital.

*Mang*Teban and the others were trying hard not to laugh. They were later released from the hospital after a routine examination. The next day, Lando brought them to a Filipino doctor who was to give them daily physical therapy for a month.

"Ang tagal naman (It's long)," *Mang* Teban complained after a week of therapy. *"Puwede ba pipirma na lang kami sa log book at* pretend we had the month-long therapy (Can we just sign in the logbook)?"

Lando had encountered similar clients before. They were too lazy to do the required daily routine, yet expected to get the money.

"Okay, but you have to give us a $500 cut from the money you will get," he told the old couple.

"How much will we receive?"

"Around $3,000 each."

"Di $2,500 na lang ($2,500 only) if we do not go everyday to the clinic?"

"Yes."

"Okay," *Mang* Teban agreed. "It's a better deal than we miss our classes at the casino."

The couple was asked to sign the log book twenty times, covering the remainder of the one month therapy.

"Bakit may laktaw ito (How come there are spaces in-between)?" *Mang* Teban asked, looking at the places where he was supposed to sign.

"So that nobody will notice you didn't come here every day. The other patients will sign in those spaces. There would be a continuous list."

Mang Teban was impressed.

"Ang galing ninyo ah (You're good)," he complimented Lando.

"We thought of everything," Lando proudly told him.

"You must be making a lot of money," *Mang* Teban said thoughtfully.

"More than enough to shower my girlfriend with money."

Mang Teban didn't know Lando was referring to Isabel, the girl from Gagalangin, Tondo whom he pretended not to know when earlier asked by the old man.

AFTER A MONTH, the couple was brought to the law office where Lando worked to receive their checks.

"Ang dali lang pala (It's easy)," *Mang* Teban said. He and his wife *Aling* Munda were excited to receive the money. The casino was waiting and they were ready for a hot streak!

"Puwede bang magpa-aksidente uli (Can I have an accident again)?" he asked.

Lando smiled at the greedy old man.

"We'll wait for while, *baka mahalata tayo* (we might get noticed)."

Everyone who worked in that office already had fake accidents and had already collected compensations from the insurance companies, sometimes more than once.

"If you know of anybody who had an accident, refer him to me. I will give you a $300 referral fee," Lando told the couple.

"Are you a lawyer?" *Mang* Teban asked him.

"No, I am not. But I work for one who signs everything and makes sure we are not caught."

The couple was very pleased. On their way home aboard Lando's car, he could not help but tell his secret to the elderly couple. Lando had become so close to them that he wanted to impress them.

"Do you remember the Isabel Mendoza from Gagalangin, Tondo, whom you asked me about the first time we met?" he asked.

"Yes," *Mang* Teban recalled.

"She's my girlfriend."

Mang Teban was surprised.

"Then you are the one caught with her in a motel by her husband?" he asked Lando.

Lando didn't expect the old man to know about the incident. He thought *Mang* Teban was just a mere acquaintance of Isabel and would not be privy to the scandal. Now he was forced to admit it.

"Yes."

"Ang hina mo naman, bakit ka nagpahuli (You are not good, why did you let yourself be caught)?"

Lando felt insulted.

"I allowed it," he proudly confessed. "In fact, I was the one who called the husband so he would break up with his wife."

"Ang galing mo pala (Then you are good)."

"Don't tell anybody," Lando warned the old couple. "This will be our closely-guarded secret."

"We won't," the old man promised.

BUT *MANG* TEBAN COULD HARDLY WAIT to break his vow. That evening, he immediately told his son Romy about Lando's admission while they were eating dinner at the apartment.

"Can you believe that guy?" *Mang* Teban said. "He doesn't have much of an education but he is very clever. I am sure he will come up with more money-making schemes for us."

Unknown to them, Ditas was cleaning the kitchen nearby. She was shocked by what she overheard, that it was Lando himself who called Isabel's husband so they would be caught.

27

A Woman's Fury

The next day, Ditas waited until her break before telling her cousin what she had overheard about Lando between her husband and father-in-law during dinner the previous night.

"*Kumusta ka na, Ate* (How are you, *Ate*)?" Ditas asked Isabel while they were having coffee.

"*Okay lang* (I'm okay)," Isabel answered. "*Kahit papano, nakakaraos* (I am surviving)."

"Don't worry, I'm sure God will hear your prayers. You'll eventually reconcile with your husband."

"I agree," Isabel replied. "I now have a strong faith God will grant my wish. If it will take a while, that's okay. Maybe I need to suffer more for my sins. As long as Albert and I will eventually end up together again, I'll be happy."

"You will," Ditas agreed.

"In fact," Isabel continued. "I dreamt about it last night. I dreamt Albert forgave me, we reconciled, and I was very happy the rest of my life."

Ditas smiled. Now that Isabel was in a better mood, she thought it would be the right time to tell her what she had discovered.

"You know what, *Ate*?" she asked. "My parents-in-law seem to be involved in a shady business deal."

"Did they cheat at the casino?" Isabel inquired.

"No, they got involved in an insurance scam."

"What happened?"

"A syndicate arranged a fake accident for them so they could collect money from an insurance company."

"That's horrible," Isabel was shocked. "No wonder our insurance premiums keep increasing – it's because of crooks like them! How much did they get?"

"About $3,000 each," Ditas answered. "And guess who the leader of the syndicate is?"

"Who?"

"Your ex-boyfriend, Lando."

"I knew it! So that's where the money came from. He's involved in illegal activities. Maybe that's why he pulls away whenever I mention the police. It makes sense now; Lando doesn't want to be booked because his records could then come out."

Ditas waited for a few moments before telling Isabel the *coup de grace*.

"And you know what?" she asked her cousin again. "I overheard Romy and his father talking about the incident at the motel. My father-in-law said Lando admitted to him it was he who called Albert and told him about your tryst. He wanted to break you and Albert apart. Lando set up everything."

Isabel's blood pressure shot up. She was outraged.

"Ang putang nang iyon, sinira ang buhay ko (That son of a bitch! He destroyed my life)."

"Relax *ka lang Ate, Bahala na ang Diyos sa kanya* (Just relax, Ate. God will take care of him).

But Isabel could not be appeased. She was livid. She wanted to hit Lando's face with a metal bat and beat him to a pulp. Lando had done so much damage to her, and nothing could possibly repay what she had lost. Without saying a word, Isabel got her handbag inside her locker and left the store.

"*Ate*," was all what Ditas could say before her cousin stormed outside.

Isabel boarded her car and drove towards National City, her destination was Lando's office about four miles away.

"Putang na! Putang na! Putang na (Son of a bitch, son of a bitch, son of a bitch)!" she kept saying as she drove on the freeway. She was not holding a metal bat when she got out of the car in front of Lando's office, but she might as well have. She was prepared to throw everything at Lando once she saw him.

"Walanghiya ka (You're shameless)!" Isabel shouted upon seeing Lando in the small law office with four desks facing the door. There were two other employees and three clients discussing some cases quietly. Lando had been seated behind his desk talking intently to an elderly lady when he saw Isabel storm inside.

Isabel walked towards Lando and began hitting him with her fists.

"Walanghiya, walanghiya, walanghiya! (Shameless, shameless, shameless)," she kept shouting.

"Stop!" Lando shouted as he tried to protect himself from the assault. He grabbed hold of one of her arms: "Why, what did I do?"

All the people in the office -- the employees and the clients -- were looking at them, shocked at what they were seeing.

"Walanghiya ka (You shameless)," Isabel railed. "You called my husband while we were in the motel room to break us apart. How could you do this to me?"

By that time, other people in the building began peeking into the office to witness the confrontation. They were amused by what they heard. This would surely make for a great scandal.

"I did not!" Lando lied.

"You're a liar! You told *Mang* Teban all about it yesterday!"

But still, Lando kept denying the accusations. The more he denied it, the more Isabel grew angrier. Embarrassed in front of his co-workers, clients and other people, Lando stormed out of the office and rushed into his car. Isabel chased after him; she would not be denied this confrontation. She refused to let him go as she kept railing at him.

"You are evil. You destroy people's lives. You are faking accidents to cheat insurance companies. You should be brought to jail!" she yelled within hearing distance of everyone. The onlookers were amused, yet somewhat astonished by these accusations. Lando noticed it and was

173

embarrassed. He felt they too were mocking him and was now growing concerned about being exposed.

Before he could start the car, Isabel managed to open the door at the passenger's side and jumped inside.

"Walanghiya ka, bakit nakarating ka pa dito sa Amerika, maninira ka lang pala ng buhay ng tao (You shameless, Why did you come here to America, just to destroy people's lives)?"

Lando was so mad and ashamed. He drove out of the street as fast as he could, with Isabel still in the car wailing at him. He wanted to escape the contemptuous looks of people behind. He entered a ramp and merged with the freeway traffic.

"*Walanghiya* (Shameless)," Isabel continued to harangue at him.

Finally, Lando responded.

"Okay, I admit it. I called up your husband because I wanted us to be caught. I wanted to break the two of you apart. Are you happy now?"

Isabel got angrier and hit him more.

"Why would you ever do that?" she asked.

"Don't you get it? *Tinaihan niya ako sa ulo noong inagaw ka niya sa akin, kaya tinaihan ko din siya* (He shat on my head when he took you away from me, and I shat on his head in return)."

"But it's not Albert's fault. He didn't even know you existed. Why did you have to include him in your revenge?"

"Because he was the cause of my troubles."

"That's not true. I would have left you even without Albert because you had no ambition in life. I kept telling you to join the U.S. Navy but you kept ignoring me. You have hurt the man I love. And you've hurt me too."

In anger, Isabel hit Lando once more. In trying to avoid the attack, Lando lost control of the car. It hit the concrete divider in the middle of the freeway and at 65 miles per hour, it rolled over two times. At least three other cars smashed into it before it stopped on the rightmost lane. The vehicle finally ended up on its side, its wheels still turning.

28

Realized Dreams

"Albert, Albert," these were the words Isabel uttered when she woke up from coma.

"*Ate, ate, si Ditas ito* (It's Ditas),"

Isabel slowly opened her eyes. Her vision was blurry at first until the face of Ditas appeared before her.

"What happened?" she asked.

"You were in an accident with Lando. You've been unconscious for the past five days."

"Where's Albert?"

She didn't bother to inquire about Lando.

"He was here about an hour ago. He went home to shower and catch some sleep. Albert was supposed to return this afternoon to take my place in watching over you."

"Is he mad?"

"No, he's not. In fact, he has forgiven you."

Tears flowed down Isabel's eyes.

"Take it easy and rest. We need you to get better," Ditas advised her.

By then, a nurse had been summoned and a doctor came in afterwards to check her condition.

"You're okay, Mrs. Mendoza," the doctor told her. "Just rest. You're not out of the woods yet."

ALBERT WAS AWAKENED BY the call from Ditas.

"Come over, Isabel is now awake," she told him.

Albert jumped from the bed and dressed up. He rushed to the hospital like a boy ready to receive a gift.

"Albert, I'm so sorry for everything," Isabel told him upon seeing her husband.

"That's okay, rest and get well soon."

Albert leaned over his wife and caressed her hair. She was crying softly.

"I didn't want to do it. I just had to get out of the situation so we could move on with our lives."

"I know, I know. Ditas told me everything including your gambling problem. You made a bad decision, several actually, but I have forgiven you."

"I have reformed, Albert. I am now a better person. I now work at McDonalds and am at peace with God."

"Yes, of course," Albert agreed and kissed her lips.

ISABEL FOUND OUT LATER Lando had died in the accident. She closed her eyes and uttered a prayer for his soul. She also asked for forgiveness for she knew she was the cause of the accident.

"As soon as you're well, we'll take that trip to the East Coast," Albert announced.

"We could fly. That would be easier," Isabel suggested.

'I know, but I've long wanted to take the road trip with you. I wanted you to see the real America."

"But you've already taken the trip by yourself. You'll just be bored."

"Isabel, I was crying and drunk half of the way," he joked. "It was no fun. I don't even remember half of it."

They both smiled.

"Let's go home to the Philippines instead. I want my parents to see us."

"If that's what you want, your wish is my command."

Isabel happily closed her eyes. She wanted to talk to Albert more, see his forgiving smile, hear his soothing voice, but her body was summoning her to rest and sleep. Immediately, the events of the past few days flashed in her mind. One was her dream the night before the accident, the dream where Albert had forgiven her and the two reconciled. How prophetic this dream came to be. If only her happiness would last as long as she lived, all of the events foretold in the dream would be realized. And they were. As she dreamt, she thought she had remained happy the rest of her life.

IT WAS A WEIRD FEELING. She was conscious all the time. She could see everything happening around her, but

178

her eyes were closed. She could not move her body, but her spirit floated in the air. Isabel could see Ditas and Albert having coffee at the hospital's canteen when they were summoned to her room and informed of her death. The two were shocked. Ditas was sobbing on the shoulders of Albert who was consoling her and caressing her back in turn. Albert tried to be strong, but could not help but also weep.

"Natupad lahat ang panaginip niya (Her dreams were realized)," Ditas told Albert once she regained control of herself.

"Anong panaginip (What dreams)?"

She told him the three-part dream of her cousin: that Albert would forgive her; they would reconcile; and she would be happy the rest of her life.

"Indeed, she lived very happy up to her last breath after you had forgiven and reconciled with her," she told Albert.

The two shuddered at the eerie thought. They knew since God had granted Isabel's last wishes, she had been forgiven for her sins and was now in heaven to enjoy eternal life.

LOOMING IN THE MIDST AS A SPIRIT, Isabel felt helpless upon seeing her family's shock and despair when learning of her death. Her mother was crying uncontrollably while her father tried to compose himself.

"I will be flying home with her as soon as everything is arranged," Albert told his father-in-law over the phone.

The old man was about to break down. Little did Albert realize he was about to grant Isabel's last wish, that they return to the Philippines so her parents could see them again.

IN TWO DAYS, Albert arrived with the remains of his wife. He made the funeral arrangements, holding the wake at an expensive funeral home in Quezon City, far away from the slum Isabel grew up in. Albert also had her interred in a memorial park. He made sure there would be two other plots beside her so she would be with her parents when their time came. This was a heart-wrenching experience for everyone, even Isabel.

"It was an accident. It could happen to anybody, anywhere, any time," Albert consoled Isabel's mother who felt guilty for prodding Isabel to seek her fortune in America. Albert chose not to tell Isabel's family about her gambling problem and the motel scandal; instead, these would be secrets that he and Ditas would keep to themselves. For that, Isabel felt grateful. Her reputation would remain intact, at least in the eyes of her family, especially her father. Albert even gave Isabel's parents $25,000.

"They were her savings," he told them. "I promised her to give them to you."

He was of course lying but knew Isabel would have been pleased with his generosity. Isabel was even surprised by the extent of her husband's kindness.

For the first time, Isabel's mother did not think of shopping after receiving the American dollars. Isabel's father put the money in a bank, never to be touched unless there were a family emergency. That was the least they could do for the hard work and sacrifices of their beloved daughter, at least in their minds.

"DON'T BE A STRANGER," Isabel's father told Albert when the time came for him to leave. "Visit us whenever you're back here in the Philippines. You are, after all, our son."

"I will," he told the old man. He hugged him and could not help but cry.

As he looked around the shanty where Isabel had been raised, he could not help but remember the first time he set foot in the place. Isabel had opened the door wearing a loose *daster* (house dress) but still looked very beautiful, much more beautiful than in her photo which Ditas had showed in America. Albert had travelled thousands of miles just to see her, prodded not by his mind but by his heart. Against the advice of his friends and even his promise to himself not to marry a girl in need of a green card, he threw caution to the wind and gave marriage another try, simply because he met and fell in love with this beautiful girl.

Albert remembered when Isabel smiled upon seeing him as she awkwardly led him to one of the two chairs in the small living room. Seated beside a window with a small round table between them, he could see the contrast between the squalor of poverty outside the house and the beauty of the girl in front of him. She was embarrassed by her poverty, but that made her much more appealing to him. He remembered their trip to Boracay and their romantic evening on the beach which led to a quickie wedding, thanks to the mischievous plot of her scheming mother.

Then he thought of her arrival in America; her wide-eyed look upon seeing her at the Los Angeles International Airport; her confusion when the waiter asked how she wanted the steak cooked; the awe and childlike expression on her face upon visiting Universal Studios and Disneyland; and

181

how excited she was to receive the red Honda car with a ribbon on its front bumper as a birthday present.

The shanty had never looked forlorn and desolate to him until now, for there was no beautiful Isabel to make it a happy place any longer.

With a heavy heart, Albert hugged his crying mother-in-law, waved goodbye to his wife's siblings, and walked on the plank of wood above the dirty water and into the street to catch a cab to the airport and away from this squalor and poverty. Isabel was heartbroken.

ISABEL TRIED TO OPEN HER EYES but she could not. She was stiff frozen and felt helpless. She summoned all her strength and tried to get loose of the imaginary sheet wrapped around her body. She exerted one hard push and finally broke loose. She was catching her breath, gasping for air, as she rose and sat on the bed. She looked around and saw Albert fast asleep. He was seated beside, his head resting uncomfortably on his arm on the bed. Once she regained her composure, Isabel savored the fresh air around. She was grateful to be alive. She laid down and reached for Albert's hand. She put it on her lips, tenderly kissing it.

"What's wrong?" Albert was awakened.

"Nothing," she said. "I just love you. I love you very much."

He smiled.

She did not bother to tell him she had just awakened from a bad dream.

29

Mikaela

Ditas was cleaning up in the kitchen when the door bell rang at seven in the evening. Her husband was with his parents in the living room watching T.V. lazily.

Romy opened the door and saw a little girl and a Mexican woman standing in front of him.

"Are you Romeo Angustia?" the woman asked him.

"Yes," he replied.

The woman introduced the little girl as Mikaela. She said the girl was the daughter of her friend, a prostitute in Tijuana who recently died of AIDS. The girl's father was identified as one of the prostitute's customers named Romeo Angustia. The Mexican woman stated that the woman had identified Romeo by his bean-sized mole at the back of his ear. Shortly before the mother was about to die, she launched a frantic search for the girl's father so she could entrust her to him. She asked some Filipino sailors frequenting the brothel and was told about a Filipino sailor with that distinct mole behind his ears. He was identified as Romeo Angustia, whom she later tracked down through the San Diego phone book.

"But I'm not that girl's father!" Romy protested.

"Can you turn your head so I could see the back of your ear?" she asked.

Romy didn't have too. He knew he had a bean-sized mole mentioned by the woman. When he refused, she forcibly put her hand at the back of Romy's ear and felt the mole. That was enough.

"Here's your daughter, take care of her. We do not have the means to do so," she said. She handed him an envelope containing the girl's birth certificate.

"No I won't," Romy refused.

"Wait here, I'll get something in the car," the woman said. She turned around and walked towards the car. She went in and drove away.

"Wait!" Romy called her. "Come back."

But she was gone.

"Who are you?" Romy asked the girl.

The girl didn't answer. She just stared blankly at Romy.

"Who's that?" Romy's father asked from the inside of the apartment.

"It's some little girl."

Ditas got curious and went to the door. The little girl was just staring at them.

"Who are you?" Romy asked in a loud voice.

The girl began to cry. Ditas took pity on her. She squatted before her and softly said: "Don't cry. What's your name? Why are you here?"

184

The girl didn't answer. She seemed not to understand English.

"Como se llama (What's your name)?" Ditas asked in Spanish.

"Mikaela," the girl shyly replied.

Romy told Ditas what the woman just said. Ditas was also surprised.

"Come in," she led the girl inside.

The night was cold.

"Don't let her in. She might be somebody else' child. We might get sued," *Mang* Teban warned her.

Ditas ignored him as Romy stood quietly looking at the child. She placed the girl on the sofa.

"Is this your daughter?" Ditas asked her husband.

"No way," Romy answered.

By then, his parents became curious and gathered around the girl.

"But the woman said so," Ditas noted.

"There might be a lot of Romeo Angustias in America," he replied.

"But no one else has a mole at the back of the ear like yours."

Romy was speechless.

He then told his parents what the Mexican woman said.

"*Hindi puwedeng maging anak mo iyan, anak ng puta iyan* (She can't be your child. She's a child of a bitch)," his father said afterwards.

"*Tatay* (Father)!" Ditas sharply cautioned her father-in-law. "Watch your language!"

Romy remained quiet. Later, he said: "How can I be her father when I can't even bear a child. I got sick remember?"

He had to remind his wife that due to his frequent visits to the brothels in Tijuana, he was afflicted with a venereal disease that caused him to be impotent.

"When did the doctors discover your ailment?" Ditas asked Romy.

"About four years ago."

"She could have been conceived before you got sick."

"*Cuantos anos tiene usted* (How old are you)," Ditas asked the girl in her broken Spanish.

"*Cinco,*" Mikaela replied nervously.

"Hey Ditas, don't implicate my son to that girl," *Aling* Munda, Romy's mother, cautioned her daughter-in-law.

"No matter, someone needs to take care of her. She's a little girl," Ditas said.

"Don't take her, bring her to the police," *Aling* Munda insisted.

"But it's already late in the evening. Besides, there's a chance she might be Romy's child."

"How will you know?"

"We'll have a DNA test taken later."

Aling Munda was about to protest when Romy told her to shut up.

"Stop it mother, let's just have her tested tomorrow," he said.

Ditas looked at the girl. She was beautiful with Mexican features. Ditas could sense some Filipino traits in her. She looked like a Mexican Shirley Temple, with curly hair, beautiful eyes, and sharp nose despite being dirty and disheveled.

"Come on, sit here," she led Mikaela to the dining table. She could sense the girl was hungry; however, the child could not understand Ditas.

"Maybe she only speaks Spanish," Ditas said aloud.

Romy was still confused. He tried to recall his escapades in nearby Tijuana five years ago, but there were far too many of them for him to remember. He was a new recruit in the Navy then, and he was like a child in a candy store. There was no way he would ever remember the identity of the girl's mother.

"Is there a photo of her mom in the envelope?" he asked Ditas.

"No," she replied.

Ditas heated a bowl of soup, rice and a piece of leftover fried chicken. The girl gobbled them down as though she had not eaten for days.

Romy watched his wife feed Mikaela. His father stood up from the sofa, looking over at the girl in disgust.

"I don't feel like watching T.V. anymore", he said, walking towards their room with his wife.

"Quiet," his wife cautioned him. "She might be our granddaughter."

"So what?" *Mang* Teban asked. *"Makakahati pa natin iyan sa grasya ng anak mo pag kinupkop dito iyan* (She might get a share of the bounty we receive from our son if she lives here)."

Ditas and Romy could not believe what they heard. *Mang* Teban didn't seem to care if the girl was his granddaughter. Even his wife seemed shocked by his insolence.

After feeding the girl, Ditas asked Romy to watch her.

"Where are you going?"

"I'll go to Savon's. It's open twenty-four hours. I'll buy her toothbrush, some clothes and other things she might need."

Mikaela had arrived with nothing but the clothing she was wearing.

Romy did not say a word. He was still confused. He stared at the girl who was quietly seated on the sofa. Then his fatherly instinct led him to change the channel of the T.V. to a Spanish station. The girl's eyes lit up and relaxed watching the station.

DITAS GAVE THE GIRL A BATH upon her return. She shampooed her hair and combed it afterwards. She led her to the sink to brush her teeth, put a new nightwear on her, and was about to tuck her to bed when Romy stopped her.

"Don't let her sleep in our bed. She might have a disease," he told his wife.

Ditas was appalled by the insensitivity of Romy considering he might be the child's father. And even if he weren't, how could he be so cruel to an innocent child? She spread a blanket on the floor, put a pillow on it and motioned to the girl to sleep there. When Mikaela was hesitant to do so, Ditas got a pillow for herself and slept beside her.

30

Gift from Heaven

Romy and Ditas took the day off the next day to attend to the needs of Mikaela. They brought her to the social welfare service office and explained how the little girl landed in their care. A social worker was assigned to the case. DNA tests for the girl and Romy were scheduled to prove or disprove his paternity. Under the law, Mikaela would have normally gone into the custody of foster parents while the paternity was sorted; however, Ditas was eager to care for her. Romy was with the U.S. Navy, and she had a well-paying job; therefore, they could provide a stable family environment for the little girl. The social worker agreed to give the couple temporary custody until the case was resolved.

"Sana anak mo nga si Mikaela (I hope Mikaela is your daughter)," Ditas told her husband as they left the agency. *"Para makumpleto ang pamilya natin* (So our family will be complete)."

Romy felt guilty. Because of his earlier indiscretions, he had gotten sick and permanently damaged. He could never have a child, which was one of the reasons why he had been resentful of his wife. He could not be a complete husband to her and to cover up for this inadequacy, he played the role of a macho and domineering husband, denying his wife the love he had professed to her, the kind he had promised her during his courtship.

He too was hoping Mikaela was his child. It would be his best chance to become a father, taking care of his own flesh and blood instead of adopting a stranger's child. But until a paternity test would prove so, he was withholding his love and affection for the little girl, one his own father labeled as *anak ng puta* (child of a bitch).

But not Ditas. She had bestowed unconditional love to the little girl from the day she realized there was a chance she could raise her as her own. It was ironic that while she could be resentful of Mikaela; instead, she was the one eagerly pursuing the girl rather than her husband. She had long been resigned to the fact that she could only be an adoptive mother despite being biologically capable of bearing her own child. Ditas had been raised to stick to her marital vow of never leaving or separating from her spouse, and now a child had landed on her lap, one whom her husband could truly love if proven to be his. Ditas didn't have to worry about herself because her good nature was capable of generously bestowing love and affection to anyone, no matter what.

"Hulog siya ng langit sa atin (She's a gift from heaven)," she told her husband who was still withholding judgment until the final ruling. But in her heart, Ditas was already convinced: Mikaela was her daughter. Like she had said, Ditas believed she's a gift from heaven, granted through the intercession of her deceased father. This was why she even bore his name, "Miguel", the Spanish and male version of "Mikaela".

Romy dropped them off at the McDonald's that Ditas was managing so the she could make sure everything in the restaurant was okay while she was away. He then proceeded to his office to work.

"NAKU, ANG GANDA NG BATANG IYAN (That child is beautiful)," Ditas' Filipina co-workers were enthused to see the child. *"Pag laki niya, dalhin mo sa Pilipinas. Tiyak kukuning artista iyan* (When she grows up, take her to the Philippines. Surely they will get her as a movie star),"

Ditas was all smiles. She was very happy, happier than she had been in quite some time. Her dream of becoming a mother could be fulfilled. Her maternal instincts could be satisfied.

She gave Mikaela a Happy Meal, a feast she eagerly devoured in minutes. The girl had some kind of appetite. In a short time, despite their inability to communicate with each other as the girl could only speak Spanish unlike Ditas, the two had bonded like mother and child.

"Take care of the restaurant," she told her co-workers afterwards. "I need to shop for clothes for Mikaela."

Ditas and the girl proceeded to the nearby mall which was just walking distance away. She brought Mikaela the clothes and other things she needed at Target's and treated her to ice cream afterwards. She even got Mikaela a doll of her choice. Ditas was like a little girl herself, dressing up her own doll, this precious little angel that had only recently entered her life. Mikaela received as much love and attention in a single day as she ever had – she never received this kind of affection in the brothel where she was born and raised. Ditas enrolled the girl in a daycare center nearby her workplace. Romy's parents refused to take care of her during the day, which may have been for the best since Ditas did not completely trust them around the girl anyway.

"SHE'S YOUR CHILD, SHE'S OUR CHILD!" Ditas happily announced to Romy as soon as he came home from work a few weeks later. She had just received the results of the DNA tests proving Romy was Mikaela's biological father. Romy could not believe the turn of events. A few weeks ago, he had no hope of ever becoming a father. In an instant, a daughter landed on his doorstep, his own flesh and blood. All the while, he didn't know he had a daughter being raised in poverty in a Tijuana brothel during the past five years. While he surely missed out on her birth and early upbringing, Romy was grateful he had found his child. It was never too late to catch up.

Romy, however, did not change from his errant ways overnight. While becoming a father had stoked the paternal instinct in him, his treatment of his martyred wife remained the same. He was still too proud to show the eternal affection he promised Ditas when wooing her a lifetime ago. This behavior persisted until he discovered a letter that forever changed the course of their relationship.

31

Letter

The letter was tucked innocently in Ditas' handbag. Romy was looking for coins to be used in his office vending machines and peeked into the bag. Ditas was taking a shower at that time, preparing for work.

It was unsealed, addressed to Ditas' mother in the Philippines and ready to be mailed with postage. Disrespecting his wife's privacy, Romy took out the letter and read it.

In it, Ditas wrote:

"Dear Nanay,

How are you doing? Have you been taking your medicine and going to your doctor's appointments? Don't worry about Mario and Lucio. My brothers are old enough to live their own life and seek their own future. I am glad they have been accepted to work as merchant marines. That would mean better pay for them and a better life, although I understand your worry because they would be working outside the country and far away from you. I will make sure you won't be alone and somebody will take care of you. I will hire a private nurse and a maid to help and accompany you.

God willing, I may be able to visit you soon. Just take care of yourself and stay healthy.

Don't believe the tsismis (rumor) of our balikbayan (returnee from abroad) townmate that Romy and his parents are mistreating me. It is far from the truth. They love me so much and have been taking care of me. In fact, during my last birthday, Romy brought me to Los Angeles to visit Disneyland, Universal Studios, and he showed me around town. He is a perfect husband and I could not ask for more.

I have more good news. You are now a grandmother. Romy found his five-year old child named "Mikaela" and we have adopted her as our own. She is very beautiful. Sabi nga ng mga kasamahang kong Pilipina sa trabaho, puwede ko daw dalhin diyan at gawing artista (My Filipina co-workers said I can take her to the Philippines to become a movie star). And you know what? Kapangalan pa siya ng Tatay (She is father's namesake). That is why I sincerely believe she's a gift from heaven, given to us through Tatay's intercession. We know because of his ailment, Romy can't give me a child.

Take care and stay healthy. May awa ang Diyos na balang araw magkakasama uli tayo (God will have pity and pretty soon, we will be together again).

I love you, Nanay.

Ditas

Romy quietly put back the letter inside the envelope and placed it in Ditas' bag. All day, he was besieged by guilt for his maltreatment of his wife. He did not expect Ditas to lie and make him look good to her mother. She even claimed he had brought her to Disneyland and Universal Studios when in fact he hasn't taken her anywhere since she landed in America. In contrast, it was her cousin Isabel whose husband Albert would take everywhere. Meanwhile, the maltreatment Ditas had been receiving from him and his parents had been continuous since day one.

He remembered the time when he was growing up. Ditas, his neighbor, had been the object of his affection since high school. But she would have nothing to do with him. He had no ambition then and was always hanging out with friends. When Ditas said she wouldn't even marry him if he were the last man on earth, he had been hurt and left town. He eventually joined the U.S. Navy, and when he returned, he found Ditas in a dire predicament. She needed money to take care of her sick mother, and through the prodding of her relatives, she was forced to marry him. At first he thought that was good enough for him. But her hurtful statement "she would not marry him even if he was the last man on earth" kept ringing in his ears despite her being a good wife, one who let him take certain liberties with whenever he pleased. And yet, this has not been good enough. He could not erase in his mind the belief she married him not out of love but necessity. This was despite the fact she lived up to her marital vows of being a loyal wife, one who would attend to all his needs as long as she lived, one who promised to remain his partner for life.

What added to his resentment, although it was not Ditas' fault, was his inability to have a child due to his liaisons with prostitutes in Tijuana. This feeling of inadequacy and his perceived lack of love from his wife had made him very insecure, prompting him to be belligerent. Instead of showering his wife with love, he maltreated her so she could feel the pain in his heart. In spite of this, however,

Ditas had remained a faithful and sacrificing wife. And now, she was even covering up for his fault by lying to her own mother and telling her he had been a good and loving husband all along. Moreover, the fact she willingly took in and loved his own daughter as her own made Romy feel so guilty and ashamed of his behavior.

"Sana anak mo siya, para mabuo na ang pamilya natin (I hope she's your daughter so we can complete our family)," Romy could remember Ditas telling him after they left the Social Welfare Office.

All along, he thought Ditas would eventually resent his abuses and give up on the marriage. Her letter proved to him she was in the marriage for the long haul, till death do them part, as they pledged in their marital vow.

AS USUAL, ROMY WENT OUT DRINKING with his friends that evening. It was a Friday night and they planned to bar hop and hopefully pick up some girls. But he felt uneasy and uncomfortable. His thought was not with the pretty white woman trying to engage him in a conversation, but rather with Ditas and how she had sacrificed so much for him and his parents. And there he was, enjoying himself and unmindful of his responsibilities as a husband – and now father. What was he doing there? He had a life, a family: why was he talking to this drunk woman who kept slurring words and laughing at random moments. At around eleven in the evening, he could not ignore his guilty feeling anymore. He pushed the drunk girl away and told his friends he would go home.

"Why? It's still early. I thought we would drink and have fun until the sun comes up," his partner-in-crime asked

"I don't feel well," he excused himself.

He went straight home and found their apartment dark. Everyone had retired to bed.

He quietly opened their room and in the dark saw the shadows of his wife and daughter sleeping on the floor. He removed his shoes and street clothes and instead of going to bed, he got his pillow and placed it beside Ditas who was lying sideways, cuddling with his daughter. He laid down beside her and put his arm around her waist. Ditas was awakened as she felt his arm and his breath behind her ears.

"I love you," he whispered to her. "I love you very much."

Ditas was surprised. She thought she was dreaming. Romy had not uttered those words since they got married. He had never been that intimate with her. Even when he made love with her, he seemed distant and aloof, sometimes belligerent, certainly never caring. She didn't say a word.

"I'm so sorry. I'm sorry for what I have done to you. I swear I'll make up for my bad behavior," Romy continued.

Ditas could not believe what she heard. He must be drunk, she told herself as she could smell beer in his breath.

"Will you forgive me?" Romy asked her as he lifted his head to see her face.

Ditas looked at him. She still was not sure if he was joking.

"Will you?" he asked again.

"There's nothing to forgive," she finally answered,

"I know you may not believe me now, but I will make you happy from now on," her husband promised. "Things are going to be better, I promise."

Ditas was pleased with the words but was not expecting much. She still thought his behavior was influenced by alcohol and the next day he would go back to being the same old Romy. He probably wouldn't even remember what he said.

32

A Changed Man

The aroma of bacon coming from the kitchen awoke Ditas. It was early Saturday morning. Ever since her daughter, Mikaela, came to her life, she had cut her working hours. She was now free on weekends and worked only an 8-hour shift, from eight in the morning to five in the afternoon. This way, she would have time to attend to her daughter in the evenings and on weekends.

She stood up and walked towards the door, leaving the little girl still sleeping on the floor. She saw Romy cooking breakfast. He walked towards her, with a ladle in his hand and kissed her on the lips. Ditas didn't know how to react. She felt awkward, and confused. It was the first time Romy showed affection, aside from the loving words he uttered last night. She tried to act normal.

"What are you cooking?" she asked.

"Bacon and eggs," he said. "I'll make pancakes and fried rice too."

"Can I help?" she asked.

"No, just sit there and be my queen for the day. I am at your employ."

Ditas didn't realize her usually belligerent husband could be that animated towards her. She wanted to tease him and tell him he was behaving corny, but she was still not comfortable enough with his amorous demeanor. She set the table and prepared to brew coffee.

"I'll take you to San Diego Zoo today," Romy announced.

Ditas was surprised.

"Why?" she asked.

"Just because," he answered.

"Whose birthday is it?" she again asked.

"Nobody," he replied. *"Gusto ko lang ipasyal ang mag-ina ko* (I just want to take out my wife and child). It's about time."

"Yes, it's about time," Ditas repeated the words to herself. But she didn't share her thoughts.

"Don't you have any appointments?" she asked him instead.

"No, and if I have, I'll cancel them. From now on, you're my priority."

Ditas felt uncomfortable. She was not used to having a pleasant conversation with her husband. It was as if she was talking to a stranger, a nice and kind-hearted stranger. She had run out of words to say. Her husband walked toward her and hugged her from behind.

"I love you," he told her. "And from now on I'm going to better show it."

Romy knew it would take a while for his wife to warm up to his new attitude and trust him. While she may not love him this time, he was determined to earn her affections no matter what. In due time, he knew she would love him in return.

When they turned around, they saw Mikaela standing in front of them. The little girl smiled.

DITAS WAS OVERWHELMED WITH HAPPINESS. She picked the girl up and kissed her.

"Nagugutom ka na (Are you hungry)?" she slowly asked her in Tagalog.

Romy walked towards them and kissed their daughter.

"Hambre usted (Are you hungry)?" he asked in broken Spanish.

The girl nodded.

"See?" he turned to his wife. "She won't understand you if you speak to her in Tagalog."

"But I want her to learn the language," she replied. "We have to talk to her in Tagalog so she can understand and speak it. That's how Mexican parents teach their kids how to speak Spanish."

"But how about in English?"

"She'll learn it when she goes to school."

"Okay," Romy turned to her daughter. *"Mula ngayon kakausapin na lang kita sa Tagalog* (From now on I will only speak to you in Tagalog)."

The girl flashed her beautiful smile.

"*MUKHANG NAGBAGO ANG IHIP NG HANGIN* (The direction of the wind seems to have changed)," *Mang* Teban, Romy's father, told his wife, *Aling* Munda after they had finished breakfast. "*Ano ba ang pinakain ng malandi mong manugang sa asawa niya at nagbago ang anak mo* (What did your flirty daughter-in-law feed to her husband - your son seems to have changed)?"

Aling Munda remained quiet.

"*Pati na ang apo mong anak ng puta, makaka-agaw pa natin sa pagmamahal ng anak mo* (Even your granddaughter who is a child of a bitch will compete with us for the affection of our son)."

"*Tumigil ka na nga diyan, Teban. Apo mo iyon, sarili mong laman at dugo* (Stop it, Teban. She's your grandchild, your own flesh and blood)!" *Aling* Munda snapped at her husband.

The old man was taken aback. Now he seemed to be alone in tormenting his daughter-in-law and granddaughter.

THE TRIO, ROMY, DITAS AND MIKAELA had a fun day at the San Diego Zoo. Ditas did not realize there was such a beautiful place and animals so close to her home.

"*Ang ganda nga pala talaga* (It's really beautiful)," she uttered.

"Wait till you see the other amusements parks nearby like SeaWorld, San Diego Wild Animal Park, Legoland, Disneyland and Universal Studios," Romy told her.

203

For Ditas, strolling in the park while their daughter was holding their hands in between them was satisfactory enough.

"DAAN MUNA TAYO SA COMMISSARY (Let's pass by the commissary)," Romy told Ditas as they left the Zoo later in the afternoon. "We can buy groceries."

"But I didn't bring any grocery money," she said.

Romy smiled at her.

"From now on, you won't have to spend your own money for our grocery needs," he told her. "Just keep your earnings to yourself and use them to help your mother. I will also take care of all our household expenses and give you an allowance so you can have your own savings account."

"But what about you?"

"Don't worry; I am done wasting money with those drinking clowns. I am retired from that life, from being such a louse. I will live up to my responsibilities as a husband and a father. I will take good care of the two of you. This is a new beginning for all of us and it starts now."

"Sobra naman iyon (That's too much)," Ditas couldn't find the proper words to say without sounding like she agreed with Romy's deprecating assessment of his old self.

"I should have been doing that a long time ago, when we first got married," Romy said.

FROM THE COMMISSARY, Romy brought Ditas and Mikaela to Chuck E. Cheese, a pizza parlor for kids, with games, rides, prizes, food and entertainment. It was the first time Ditas and Mikaela had ever been in such a fun place and they loved it.

"Huwag kang masiyadong kumain anak, tataba ka (Don't eat too much, child. You're get fat)," Ditas cautioned her daughter in Tagalog.

Romy and Ditas were amused with their child who consumed half of the whole pie.

"Let her have it," Romy said.

They didn't have to say it, but they knew Mikaela's big appetite was the result of her years of depravation while growing up poor in Tijuana.

"In due time, she'll get used to food and won't overeat," Romy opined.

"She better be," Ditas said. "Otherwise she can't be a movie star in the Philippines if she's fat."

The couple laughed.

"LET'S TAKE THE WEEK OFF," Romy told his wife on their way home.

"Why?"

"So we can go to SeaWorld, Legoland, Disneyland and Universal Studios."

"Won't that be too much?"

"No, we should have visited those places a long time ago. Back when I was a jackass."

Ditas smiled. She was now getting comfortable with her husband and soon she knew she would be much closer to him. The Romy of the old was quickly becoming a thing of the past.

In the meantime, she had to overcome her awkwardness towards him. They were starting all over again in a new relationship. They were like teenagers who had just gotten hitched. They were not yet used to showing complete affection towards each other. They were still uncomfortable in hugging and kissing one another; however, pretty soon, they knew they would overcome the initial shyness like everybody else. They would behave like unconditional lovers, like real husband and wife.

For her reversal of fortune, Ditas knew she only had God to thank. She had prayed for a long time to her patron saint, the Mother of Perpetual Help, for her husband to change his illicit ways. And her prayers were finally answered. With her daughter sleeping on her lap as her husband was driving them home, Ditas could not have asked for more.

That evening, as Mikaela slept on the floor, their matrimonial bed had finally become a pleasant place for Ditas to make love with her husband.

33

Cross Country Trip

"BINGO!" *MANG* TEBAN SHOUTED after crossing out the last number in his card. It was a rare feat. It had been an hour since the game started and no one had come up with the right configuration to win. And when someone finally did, he achieved the rarest of the feats: being able to cover all the numbers in a bingo card. And this time it was *Mang* Teban.

"Diyos ko Teban, papaano mo nagawa iyan (Oh God Teban, how did you do it)?" his wife, *Aling* Munda cried in disbelief. The other players were also astounded. No one had done so since the casino was opened.

"I can't believe it myself," *Mang* Teban exclaimed.

A bingo official examined the winning card and declared *Mang* Teban's victory official.

"Finally," the old man enthused. "After years of investing thousands of dollars in this casino, I won big!"

The officials were all smiles too. They knew *Mang* Teban was one of the biggest losers in the game, yet, he persisted in playing. What he had won was just a small portion of his losses. The win, which was a difficult one, was considered a jackpot, and *Mang* Teban won much more than the regular amount of the prize money. He was told to claim his special prize at the cashier's office.

"Congratulations *Tatay*," one of the cashiers, a Filipino, greeted him. *"Heto ho ang papeles, pirmahan ninyo* (Here are the papers, sign them)."

Then one Filipino bystander asked him: "Are you receiving Social Security Supplementary Income?"

"Yes," Romy's father replied.

"Naku, delikado ho iyan, baka kuwestiyunin kayo ng Social Security System (That's dangerous. The Social Security System might question you)?"

"Bakit (Why)?"

"Your SSSI is just a supplementary income given by the government to assist you since you do not have other sources of income. It is not an SS retirement income which you would have earned after years of working. SSSI is essentially a freebie given to people who lack the minimum amount of money to cover their living expenses. You are not supposed to bet the money in the casinos; the money should only be spent on your basic needs."

"That's not right! I've been spending thousands of dollars in this casino!"

"You can get the prize, but you will be taxed and the welfare agency may stop giving you your SSSI since you already have money."

"Naku Teban, nagsusugal pala tayo sa wala (Teban, we are gambling for nothing)," *Aling* Munda told her husband.

"Mabuti palang sinunog ko na lang ang mga pinangsugal ko (It's better I burned the money I gambled)," *Mang* Teban exclaimed. "How come my other winnings were not questioned?"

"Because they were too small. This one is big and the casino has to issue an IRS 1099-Miscellaneous form to be reported to the Internal Revenue Service," said the Filipino cashier.

"Papaano iyan (What now)?" *Mang* Teban asked the Filipino guy.

"May paraan diyan (There's a way out to it)," said the bystander.

"I can sign my own name as the recipient of the winnings, provided you give me fifteen percent of the money. That way, the IRS won't know you earned that much, your taxes will be negligible, and the welfare agency people won't question you."

"Ang laki naman ng taga mo (Your cut is big)."

"But I will use part of the commission to pay the tax."

"Sige na Teban, pumayag ka na, kaysa sa wala (Just agree Teban. It's better than nothing)," his wife urged him.

"Okay," *Mang* Teban agreed.

"Masuwerte kayo at nandirito ako para saluhin kayo. Marami na akong natulungang kababayan natin na nag-SSSI at nanalo ng malaki sa casinong ito (You are lucky I am here to help. I have helped a lot of our countrymen who were on SSSI and won big in this casino).

The bystander didn't bother to tell the old man that he was always there precisely to search for such an opportunity to make extra money out of the winnings of old Filipino gamblers like *Mang* Teban who received SSSI.

Little did the Filipino bystander know his racket wouldn't pay dividends in the long run. The taxes he was told to pay for his alleged "winnings" were far greater than what he had expected. The following year, he increased the commission he was charging to cover the taxes he would pay. The bystander also found a way to shrink his tax payments by reporting false gambling losses as deductions. He continued to conspire with his elderly Filipino countrymen in committing fraud against the U.S. government and taxpayers. But his unusual big winnings and losses would generate a red flag in the IRS. It would just be a matter of time before the authorities would come knocking at his door to audit him and discover his crimes.

IT TOOK A MONTH for Isabel to fully recover from her injuries. She had to undergo physical therapy to become her old self again.

"Now we can take that cross-country trip to our home in Virginia," her husband told her.

"Why don't you join us?" Albert asked Romy and Ditas who were visiting her with their daughter Mikaela. "Then you can fly back to San Diego."

"Yes, why not?" Isabel enthused. *"Para mas masaya* (So it will be more fun)."

Romy momentarily looked at his wife and said, "Okay."

"How about my job?" Ditas asked.

"We can both take a month-long vacation. *Malakas ka naman sa boss mo* (You have a strong influence on your boss)."

"Let's go for it!" Albert declared.

THE ROAD TRIP was a chance for the women and the little girl to see America. From San Diego, they went up north to Las Vegas, Nevada; went back south to the Grand Canyon, then Phoenix, Arizona; El Paso and Dallas, Texas; passing through Louisiana and Mississippi; then crossing into Alabama; then Atlanta, Georgia; South Carolina; North Carolina; and into Virginia.

They didn't follow the shortest route. Whenever there were tourist attractions in the area, they would take a side trip to see the place.

In Las Vegas, they checked out the Hoover Dam and stayed at the Circus Circus Casino so Mikaela could enjoy the attractions for children, which in fact they all enjoyed

"Naku Ate, ang daming slot machines. *Maglaro tayo* (Hey *Ate*, there's a lot of slot machines. Let us play)," Ditas teased her cousin.

"Heh! Tumigil ka nga diyan. Isinumpa ko na ang sugal (Stop it, I already forsook gambling)," Isabel replied.

Albert and Romy both laughed.

THEY ALL MARVELED AT THE MAJESTIC SIGHT of the Grand Canyon; the Old West towns of Tucson, Arizona; walked on Dallas Pioneer Place; saw the city's

World Aquarium Exhibit; the Coca Cola Museum and Olympic Park in Atlanta, Georgia; the historic Charleston and Fort Sunter National Monument in South Carolina; the Whitewater Falls and Smoky Mountain National Park in North Carolina; the Colonial Williamsburg and Jamestown Settlement in Virginia; and other tourist attractions along the way.

They also bonded together as close friends and relatives. And they all enjoyed Mikaela, whom everyone agreed was beautiful enough to grow and become a movie star in the Philippines. The two best friends, Albert and Romy, were in the front seats alternately driving the car while the cousins, Isabel and Ditas, chatted in the back. In between them was little Mikaela, as happy as she had ever been. Romy enjoyed the trip and the bonding with his family so much that once they reached the East Coast, he suggested to his wife: "Since we're already here, let's visit the other areas nearby."

"Where should we go?" Ditas asked.

"We can tour Washington D.C., Baltimore, Philadelphia, New York City and Boston. They are all accessible by car."

"How long will it take?" Ditas asked.

"About two weeks."

"That's too long. We will lose our jobs."

"Don't worry about our jobs, I will take care of that problem," Romy told his wife.

Unknown to Ditas, her husband had a plan that would forever change the course of their lives.

34

Change of Plan

ROMY'S PLAN WAS TO TAKE his family home to the Philippines for good.

"What, we are leaving America?" Ditas asked her husband in disbelief.

"Yes," Romy replied.

"What about your naval career?"

"What naval career? I never wanted to be a navy man. I wanted to farm in the Philippines. I just joined the U.S. Navy because you drove me away and I wanted to make enough money to win you over," Romy told his wife.

Ditas was still confused.

"Why give up the opportunities and comfort here in the U.S.?" she asked.

"There are also many opportunities back home and with hard work, we can earn the same amount of money as we could here. Besides, I want you to be able to take care of your mother so you can be with her while it's not yet too late. I know how sick she is – she needs her daughter there."

Romy could still remember his wife's touching letter to her mother, her hiding his abuses and her longing to care of her mom.

Ditas could not believe what she heard. It was as though she was listening to a different man, not her husband Romy. But she could detect the sincerity in his eyes. She was overwhelmed.

"Are you kidding?" she was not yet convinced.

"Of course not," he replied. "Let's take care of your mother and I'll make sure to work extra hard to match, if not surpass, my earnings here. Besides, we already saw most of America. In the Philippines, as long as we are not poor, we'll lead a good life. Together."

"Mamasukan ka ba sa atin (Are you going to be an employee there)?" Albert asked Romy. He too had misgivings with Romy's decision.

"Of course not," replied Romy. "I have some savings. I plan to buy a piece of land, farm it and engage in other businesses."

"What businesses?"

"Whatever I can afford. Maybe I'll start with tricycles and have somebody operate them. Later, maybe passenger jeepneys."

"How much capital can you bring home?" Albert asked.

"About $10,000," Romy replied.

He knew had he not wasted his money with friends, he could have saved more. But this would still be a solid nest egg.

214

"All right," Albert said. "Let me help out. I have $50,000 I can invest in you. You buy some land, farm it, and we'll divide the profits. You'll be the industrial partner; I'll be the capitalist."

Romy accepted his friend's offer.

Ditas was overwhelmed by the turn of events as her prayers were answered again. She had been itching to go back to the Philippines to be with her mother since she knew she did not have much time left to live.

"I hope you do well," Albert said. "I also plan to retire in the Philippines in the next ten years. I am tired of life here in America. It's too fast."

"How about Mikaela?" Isabel asked. "We can no longer enjoy her company."

"Don't worry, *Ate*, you'll have your own child soon enough," Ditas assured her. "Besides, once Mikaela is grown up and a movie star, you'll get a free pass in all her movies."

The two couples had a good laugh. In their minds, however, this was a possibility. And so would be the chance their business would succeed.

"ANO? NAHIHIBANG KA NA BA? Nakahiga ka na sa kama, matutulog ka pa sa sahig (Are you a fool? You're already in bed, you still prefer to sleep on the floor)?" *Mang* Teban blurted out when his son Romy told him his plans.

"I prefer to be in the Philippines. I can be my own boss unlike here where my military officers order me around."

"How about us? Who will take care of us?" *Aling* Munda asked.

"You can do without us, *Nanay*. My sister can take care of you here."

So he thought.

But when Romy broached the idea to his sister Myra who also lived in San Diego with her family, she balked.

"No way," she said. "My husband won't agree to it."

"Why wouldn't Tony?" asked Romy.

"We already discussed it before, and he didn't want to."

"Let me talk to him."

THE FOLLOWING SUNDAY, Romy invited Tony and his family for dinner. He then told him about his plan.

"I am sorry*, kuya*, I can't let *tatay* and *nanay* stay with us," he responded.

Mang Teban and *Aling* Munda were surprised. They were always civil to their son-in-law unlike their abusive treatment of Ditas.

"Bakit naman (Why)?" Romy asked.

"I am just getting even with my wife. When my mother was staying with us, Myra was discourteous to her and treated her rudely. My poor mom chose to go back to the Philippines and live alone. My wife didn't want her to live with us – so why should I let her parents do the same?"

Romy, Myra and their parents could not speak. They knew it was their bad karma.

"Paano na kami (How about us)?" *Aling* Munda asked again.

"Why don't you get your own apartment?" Tony asked her.

"Rent is expensive these days. A studio could cost us at least $900 monthly."

"So?" Tony asked again. "The government is giving you free money in form of Social Security Supplementary Income for your living expenses after all. Use the money for your rent instead of wasting it in the casinos."

"Our SSSI is not much, only $600 for each of us."

"What do you expect? You did not work to earn this money. You should be grateful you're getting free money from taxpayers, from those who toiled hard in this country."

Romy wanted to cut-off his brother-in-law due to his disrespecting his own parents, but he knew Tony was right.

"It's good you could save on rent during the years you were staying with *Kuya* Romy. If you saved those monies, you would have plenty to spare in your retirement years," Tony added. "We all know you're breaking the law and cheating us taxpayers; we all know you're falsely reporting you're paying rent in your tax returns."

Tony was enjoying himself. He had long waited for the opportunity to tell his in-law he knew about their abuse of the American taxpayers. He also considered accusing them of abusing Ditas for all of those years but decided against it because he did not wish to embarrass his loving sister-in-law.

217

Still, Romy and Myra could not stop him because they knew Tony was telling the truth.

"How about this," Romy finally proposed. "Let my parents stay with you and they will pay you rent for the room, say $500 each month."

"*Pumayag ka na* (You agree)," Myra told her husband. "*Malaking tulong din sa atin ang $500* ($500 is a big help to us)."

"But it would be a big expense on our part," *Mang* Teban protested.

"*Pumayag ka na* (You agree)," Aling Munda also told her husband. "*Kaysa naman matulog tayo sa kalye* (It's better than we sleep in the streets)."

Grudgingly, the two men accepted the compromised proposal.

"*Kasalanan ito ng maldita nating manugang na si Ditas at ng anak ng puta nating apo* (This is the fault of our devilish daughter-in-law Ditas and our child of a bitch granddaughter)," *Mang* Teban told his wife when they were alone in their room.

Aling Munda slapped him hard on the cheek. She had enough of her unconscionable husband.

"*Apo mo iyon. Ang sarili mong laman at dugo* (She is your own granddaughter. Your own flesh and blood)," she berated him.

35

Karma

It took Romy almost a month to settle his affairs in San Diego before he could take his family home to the Philippines for good. Ditas was doubly excited not only to see her mother, but also to show off her daughter, the beautiful Mikaela.

By the time they settled in the Philippines, Mikaela could understand a bit of Tagalog due to her daily conversation with her parents. Romy turned out to be a loving father to Mikaela, the apple of his eyes. The father and daughter were inseparable, even when Romy would go to the rice fields and select the land he would buy or check out the crops being tended by his workers. They stayed in Ditas' old house with her mother at first; soon, they built their own four-bedroom house, upgraded with U.S. standard amenities, besides the old one which was torn down.

Ditas' mother and Isabel's mom inherited the property from their parents, and the rear of the lot was reserved for Isabel's parents when her father retired. But there were still fields beyond the backyard that could be used to plant vegetables and crops.

With his own and Albert's funds, Romy purchased more farmlands and jeepneys to increase the profitability of their enterprises. With proper management and a wise use of resources, the business soon prospered. In addition, Ditas put up a big store in front of the house where neighbors bought their everyday needs. Pretty soon, Romy and Ditas were making more money in the Philippines than in the United States, proving they had made the right decision.

Ditas' sickly mother recovered from her illness, what with the company of her daughter and her family. They all doted on Mikaela, who, even at a young age, showed her artistic talents. She could sing and dance beautifully to the delight of her parents, their friends and neighbors.

Romy never returned to his old errant ways and continued to be a model husband and father to his family in addition to being a good provider. With their late model car, they travelled to different places in the Philippines every now and then and enjoyed much quality family time together, an endeavor that would have been difficult had they remained in America.

"NAKU TEBAN, NAHULI SI DR. GARCIA (Hey, Teban, Dr. Garcia was caught)," *Aling* Munda nervously told her husband one day. They were staying in their daughter's and Tony's apartment. Dr. Garcia was the Filipino doctor who prescribed them the wheelchairs they didn't need, which they sold and were transported to the Philippines.

"*Ano na kaya ang nangyari kay Berto* (What happened to Berto)?" *Mang* Teban asked, looking at the news item and photo of Dr. Garcia in the newspaper. Berto was the Filipino guy who had acted as a conduit in illegally providing them the wheelchairs through the welfare assistance funds. "*Siguro nagtatago na* (Maybe he's hiding.)"

The couple's questions were soon answered when the police came knocking at their door. It seemed Berto was caught and divulged the names of the members of the syndicate, including those Filipino senior citizens who participated in the scam. The police looked for the wheelchairs given to the couple for their own use, and when the two could not show them, they were listed as among the suspects in illegally bilking the government and committing fraud.

"Diyos ko, Diyos ko, ano ba ang nangyari sa atin? Kung kailan pa tayo tumanda at saka ngayon pa tayo nagkakaso (Oh God, what happened to us? Now that we are already old, we got involved in a criminal case)," *Aling* Munda blurted out. She was very nervous and her blood pressure rose. *"Ikaw kasi, napakagahaman mo* (You are to be blamed, you are very greedy)."

"Tumigil ka na nga, ikaw din nagpasasa (You stop, You also reaped the benefits we got)," *Mang* Teban told his wife. No matter how much he tried to hide it, it was evident he too was nervous.

All the people involved in the illegal activity were rounded up and brought to court. A public defender advised them to plead guilty since the evidence was inconvertible. Because it was their first offense, *Mang* Teban and *Aling* Munda received probation but were ordered to pay back the amount of the wheelchairs, plus interest.

The experience took a toll on *Aling* Munda's health. Her blood pressure remained high stemming from her worrying about their fate. Even after the case ended, she continued to suffer from the effects of a nervous breakdown and had lost her appetite. She lost weight and even became bedridden.

But that was not the end of their troubles. When Lando's relatives sought remuneration from the accident that caused his death, the investigators discovered he had been involved in several accidents before. His illegal activities along with those of the people in his office were unearthed and cases were brought against all of them. The firm's lawyer was eventually disbarred and imprisoned. While the government could not send Lando to jail since he had died, it succeeded in freezing and eventually forfeiting all of his estate's assets. In the end, Lando's relatives did not get a single cent.

Isabel, on the other hand, received a $20,000 settlement for the injuries and other damages she suffered from the accident. At first, she wanted to return the money.

"I did not earn this," she claimed. "I was even the cause of the accident; I don't feel it is right to be rewarded for it."

"Stop blaming yourself," Albert advised her. "Get over it and accept it was an accident; It's nobody's fault."

"But if I benefit from this blood money, I might incur a bad karma."

"You can no longer return the money to the insurance agency. The insurance policy prescribed that you be awarded it as it has a no-fault provision. Just set aside the money and use it in a charitable cause when the time comes."

MANG TEBAN AND ALING MUNDA were not spared from prosecution despite their age. They were brought back to court for participating in their fake accident. This took a further toll on Aling Munda's health and before the case was resolved, she suffered a stroke that left her in a coma.

Mang Teban was forced to face the music alone. Even though he was already old, he was sentenced to a full year in prison because it was his second offense. He had used up his probation allowance the first time he committed a crime, and this new judge wanted to teach the local criminals a serious lesson, even the Filipino senior citizens. The law does not favor the aged, he reminded them.

"*Nakakahiya itong nangyari sa akin. Malalaman sa bayan namin na nakulong ako* (What happened to me is embarrassing. It will be known in our town I was imprisoned)," *Mang* Teban muttered to himself as he was led away to jail. His daughter Myra was crying as she bid her father goodbye.

Mang Teban did not complete his sentence. Quietly suffering from a deep depression, he died from a broken heart weeks before his release.

But not his wife. *Aling* Munda continued to live a long life, five more years since her stroke. She was in coma all the time though. She never woke up. The hospital attendants had to turn her over in bed every now and then to relieve the pressure on her back; otherwise, she would have received bedsores. The government spent thousands of dollars for her confinement, which the medical practitioners did not mind because they knew they could earn more money the longer their patient lived, even with this poor quality of her life.

Some argued the money spent to keep her breathing could have been better used in other endeavors considered more worthwhile, like in educating children to build a better future for the country or helping the poor to ameliorate their hardships. Public school teachers were being laid off in San Diego then for lack of funds. Still, society had not reached the point where the value of human life, no matter how frail it may seem, could be ignored.

Although *Aling* Munda's children pitied her while she remained in a state of being a living dead, they were confused, indecisive and unable to tell the doctors to pull the plug and end her sufferings.

36

Promises Fulfilled

After thirty years in government service, Isabel's father retired with the cleanest of all records. He had been steadfast in sticking to his principles of not accepting bribes and fulfilling his duties to the letter, sometimes to the detriment of his career. Often, he was bypassed for promotions because he didn't want to play along with the ploys of his superiors and other higher ups. Sometimes he was assigned minor tasks as punishment for his non-cooperation. But through it all, his high moral values reigned supreme. Until in the end, even his detractors shared the highest regard and utmost respect for him.

With his daughter Isabel in the United States and his two other children in college, he moved with his wife to the province and built a small bungalow behind the house Romy and Ditas had built. The property turned out to be an ideal place to retire; being away from the city, there was an abundance of fresh air and clean surroundings. But before settling down for retirement, Isabel and Albert arranged for her parents to visit them in the United States. Romy and Ditas joined them, bringing along Mikaela and Ditas' mother.

"*Hindi ko akalaing makakarating pa ako dito sa America* (I did not expect to be able to come here to America)," *Aling* Lucing, Ditas' mother mused when they landed at the Los Angeles International Airport. She had been near death when Ditas first left her to join her husband Romy, but through the help of her daughter's financial support and love, her good health was restored.

The group stayed for a few days in Los Angeles where they visited different attractions: Disneyland, Universal Studios, the San Diego Zoo, and SeaWorld. It was another opportunity for Mikaela, now ten years old, to appreciate better the places she had first visited as a young child.

Her parents also brought her to Tijuana, Mexico so she could have an idea of the place where she was born. In due time, they planned to tell her of her past, but not until she had attained the maturity and emotional stability they thought she needed.

They then they travelled to the East Coast where Isabel and Albert brought them to different neighboring cities, including Virginia; Washington, D.C.; Baltimore; Philadelphia; New York; and Boston. Their two-month stay in the U.S. was very enjoyable and satisfying; however, the old folks felt more comfortable living the remainder of their lives back home.

"Para sa mga bata lamang itong America (America is just for the young)," Isabel's father told his daughter when she asked if he wanted to be petitioned and migrate to the U.S. *"Maligaya na kami sa bayan natin* (We are already happy in our country)."

ISABEL MADE THE MOST of their remaining years in the U.S., knowing fully well they would retire in the Philippines in a few years time. Isabel gave birth to a son,

Albertito, but that did not prevent her from pursuing a career of her own. She became a successful insurance agent, helping young families carve out a secured future for themselves. She was active in the community, raising funds for charity, especially for causes that would help her countrymen in the Philippines. She was also involved in several major charities, making sure God did not make a mistake in sparing her life during her earlier accident. She knew she had a responsibility to help improve others' lives in exchange for her own second chance in life.

When her father broached to her the idea of putting up a brass band in their *barrio* to help the youth learn how to play musical instruments and develop positive character, Isabel donated the $20,000 (plus interest) of the insurance settlement she had received from the accident. She realized it was the charity project she had been waiting for use of the money. She did so in memory Lando, whose death she still felt guilty over. He may not have been a good man, but at least some good came from his passing and thus from him.

Her father organized the band and taught the kids to play the instruments after school hours. During special occasions, the band was asked to perform and join the parades in different festivities in the province. They were the envy of the other towns without a band because it not only gave the youth an opportunity to learn music, but it also helped develop their good character. Moreover, most of the members were able to get college scholarships as many of them would join school bands, enabling them to earn a degree and secure their future.

Romy's agricultural ventures and other businesses prospered. With help from the capital from Albert, the retained earnings of their company, plus loans from the Development Bank of the Philippines, they were able to buy more lands for their poultry and cattle operations. In addition to the jeepneys they operated, they also had five buses that transported passengers to other places.

Ditas did her share by organizing medical missions in the remote *barrios* of their town. Their once-a-year medical mission had become monthly, until it eventually became a sustainable everyday operation that attended to the health needs of the poor in their area. Proof of the positive effects of the charitable endeavor on the community encouraged friends and rich folks in their area to continue donating money and labor. Her husband and Albert's company also set aside a budget for this charitable project, which was augmented by the funds raised by Isabel in the U.S. Isabel was grateful to God for giving her a second chance in life and vowed to spend most of it helping people – these were her obligations now.

AS PROMISED, Albert retired after ten years and brought his family back to the Philippines. They bought the piece of land beside the house of Romy and Ditas and built their own house. The long-time friends had become successful business partners, as their wives joined together in pursuing their charitable works.

Mikaela lived up to her promise. She grew up into a beautiful girl, the Mexican and Filipino features blending together to turn her into a rare beauty. As predicted, she became a very popular movie star.

She appeared in a film developed from a book written by her cousin, Albertito, the son of Albert and Isabel. The movie was about two cousins who sought fortune in the U.S by marrying U.S. Navy personnel only to realize the good life they were seeking was right in their home country, the

Philippines. Mikaela played the role of the beautiful Isabel, a girl from the slums who learned the hard way that life in the Land of Milk and Honey was not as easy as it was purported to be.

The title of the movie? "Promised Land"!

It was a big hit.

(The End)

About the author

Simeon G. Silverio, Jr. was born and raised in Manila, Philippines, and was educated at the Juan Sumulong Elementary School and Arellano High School, both in Santa Cruz, Manila. He obtained his Bachelor of Arts degree in Journalism at the University of the Philippines and took graduate courses for a Master in Communications and a Master in Business Administration at the Ateneo de Manila University. He was the managing editor of Sunburst Publications, publishers of **Sunburst International Magazine**, **Business Outlook in the Philippines & Asia** and **Yaman Magazine.** He also published and edited **Business Ventures in the Philippines & Asia**. He migrated to the United States in 1982 and published and edited the **Asian Journal,** a weekly Flipino-American newspaper in San Diego from 1987 to the present. In 1999, he co-founded the **Los Angeles Asian Journal** and later moved on to focus on his business interests in San Diego, California where he lives.